A GUIDE TO THE DARK

Words and photographs by

MERIAM METOUI

HENRY HOLT AND COMPANY

NEW YORK

Content warning: This book contains depictions of drowning, suicide, violence, blood, and death.

Henry Holt and Company, *Publishers since 1866*
Henry Holt® is a registered trademark of Macmillan Publishing Group, LLC
120 Broadway, New York, NY 10271 • fiercereads.com

Our books may be purchased in bulk for promotional, educational, or business use. Please contact your local bookseller or the Macmillan Corporate and Premium Sales Department at (800) 221-7945 ext. 5442 or by email at MacmillanSpecialMarkets@macmillan.com.

Library of Congress Control Number: 2022920072

First edition, 2023
Book design by Aurora Parlagreco
Interior photographs by Meriam Metoui
Printed in the United States of America

ISBN 978-1-250-86321-8
1 3 5 7 9 10 8 6 4 2

To Norma Rahal. The words elude me.

No one ever told me that grief felt so like fear.
—C. S. Lewis

ONE

It was only a room at the time. There was nothing about it that Peter found out of place.

Eerie.

Wrong.

It was only a room in a motel in a city he never planned on coming back to. A fleeting memory, if one at all. But Peter Greenwell had the unfortunate honor of being the first.

When the phone rang, Peter was in the shower. He stood beneath the hot water, hoping it would calm his quick heartbeat. He had been waiting for this call.

Dreading it.

Either way, it was inevitable, and so he shut off the water and readied himself to face what he could no longer avoid. But as his foot found the cold tile and his hand reached for the towel with *Wildwood Motel* embroidered near the edge, Peter slipped. He scrambled for a moment, trying to find something to grab on to. But the towel slid away from the hook, and his other hand grasped only air. It all happened quicker than he thought it would. There was no time to reflect or slow down. No time for one uneventful life to flash through Peter Greenwell's mind.

His head made contact with the porcelain sink and he sank to the floor, the blood and water like tendrils delicately painting the life that seeped out of him. It was 1978, only two years after the motel had first opened its dozen rooms.

Twelve years later, Lola Moreno was next. She was only looking for some quiet, a day or two away, when she realized too late that she might be able to escape her life but not her mind. Next came Eugene McDaniel, nine years after that, a retired teacher on his way to visit two grandchildren who had all but forgotten him, and on and on it went. All the way to a Noah Davis, only four months prior, who knew of every death that had come before and the part he had played in many of them.

Room 9's history was dark and rotten and had a way of sinking into its guests. Their deaths within it were unfortunate in the same way. They all came too close to the flame, and when that happens, the fire takes care of the rest.

Tonight is no different.

TUESDAY

TWO

Layla

We were supposed to drive straight to Chicago, but it was pouring, the windshield an indecipherable picture of the road ahead. The rain had started ten minutes ago in one of those torrential downpours that appear out of nowhere. Mira slowed down, her shoulders scrunched over the steering wheel as she tried to make sense of where the lane was. It didn't help that we had taken the wrong exit a while back and my phone was refusing to cooperate. Five bars, my ass. The map app refused to load no matter how many times I restarted it.

"I think we need to pull over and wait this out, Mira. I'm pretty sure it's only getting worse."

Mira squinted at the windshield. Her brow furrowed, and then her eyes went wide. A small gasp escaped her lips before she quickly twisted the steering wheel to the right. I couldn't see what Mira swerved to avoid, but by then, it didn't matter. The tires skidded across the road, farther than she had planned.

It happened faster than either of us expected. My seat belt yanked me back, firm and sharp against my collarbone, as the car spun. It made a full turn before it slipped past the pavement and landed in a ditch, the front bumper resting against the wet dirt at an angle. On impact, the opening of the airbag compartment snapped against the windshield and shattered the glass. A thousand cracks branching out at once. Seconds later, I could feel my raw skin burn with the sudden friction of the seat belt.

The sound of rain pounding against the roof filled the small space as the smell of burnt rubber and smoke wafted in.

"Layla? Layla, are you okay?" Mira said.

There was a quiet hum, low and steady, but I couldn't tell if it was the car or in my head. I nodded, wanting to say more but managing only that. I looked back at her, relieved that she seemed fine. There was a trail of blood down her temple, dark against her skin.

"You're bleeding," I said, reaching toward her. She looked up at the rearview mirror between us and wiped it with the back of her hand.

"I'm fine. I feel fine, I promise." She smiled at me, small and reassuring, and got out to inspect the damage. The rain was loud and heavy on the windshield, but I could make out the shape of her against the car headlights. She crouched to get a better look. Even if she did have a handle on things, I felt bad watching her get drenched. It was only fair that I join her. I stepped out of the car and my flats immediately sank into the mud. This night clearly wasn't done with me yet. I trudged over to Mira, wondering how she managed to look so graceful.

"I thought I saw someone, but"—she paused, squinting through the rain—"there's nothing here."

I bent down to study the car. This looked bad. Like stranded-in-the-middle-of-nowhere bad. The right head-light was cracked, though the main bulb still shone through. The windshield had shattered, a spiderweb at the bottom spreading outward. And a flat front right tire surrounded a bent rim. There was no way Keira was drivable. We barely knew how to change a tire, if knowing in theory even counted, and this was beyond us. We were going to die out here, weren't we? Some serial killer was going to spot us on his nightly stroll, and that would be the end of us. I hoped it would be quick.

"You don't have to say it. We're screwed," Mira said.

The storm was letting up, but she looked at the sky and let the rain continue to drench her long brown curls. Her leather jacket was open, and the visible part of her gray top was soaked through, the edges of her bra outlined against the thin T-shirt.

"This is fine. We're totally fine. Just fine." My pitch rose with every word. She raised an eyebrow and smiled at my rising panic, squinting through the thinning rain.

"I'm going to go call a tow truck or something," she said.

She went back inside the car, the rain now a mist. Gone as quickly as it had come.

I sat down at the edge of the road where the grass met the pavement and lay back, letting my dress soak through. What was the point of anything? We were nearing the end of our College Tour Spring Break Best Friend Road Trip, which had been one perfectly memorable and adventure-filled week. No parents. No school. No younger sisters constantly breathing down my neck. Just Mira and me and the open road.

But we'd crashed the car in the middle of nowhere, would miss tonight's hotel reservation, and had little chance of making it to tomorrow's Undergraduate Portfolio Day at the School of the Art Institute of Chicago, what would have been the highlight of the trip, only second to spending it with Mira, of course. The ten-years-older version of me that's photographing magazine covers and working on editorial shoots was fading with each passing second. I thought of my portfolio, carefully tucked away in my bag. They'd never see it now. My best shot at getting off their waitlist, gone. I might as well take it out and let the rain soak through the thick paper. Let the ink run together until the photographs were an unintelligible mess.

Mira slammed the car door and made her way over. Our height difference felt even more exaggerated as she stood over me. Droplets fell from her sharp jaw and landed near my mud-soaked shoes. She handed me my camera bag and stretched out next to me, letting the wet grass soak through her jeans.

"Thought you might be worried about your baby. Sturdy little thing," she said. I hugged the bag to my chest and took out the camera to inspect. Thank you, past me, for actually putting it away after our last shoot in Nashville. I stood up and took a test shot just in case, framing the wrecked car in the center and letting the beams flare against the lens. I sighed in relief. Everything seemed to be working. The edge of the light took on an odd shape, but it must have been the bright headlights playing against the lens. At least one thing wasn't entirely and irrevocably ruined.

"Keira looks like a goner," I said, studying the tilt of Mira's car against the mud.

"Nah, she's sturdy too. She'll pull through." She took a deep breath and let the mist dampen her skin. She had her hazel eyes closed, her head tilted back, the edge of a smile on her lips. I snapped a quick photo of her bathed in the car

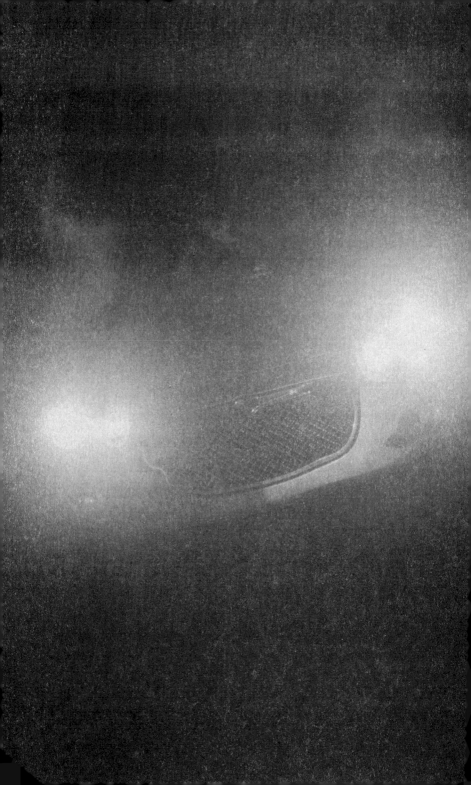

headlights and turned off the camera. Mira deserved this trip more than anyone. After the shit year she'd had, home was anything but. Things were different since Khalil, her brother, died. *She* was different. The Mira who laughed too quickly and loved too hard was gone. In her place was an impulsive, more anxious Mira. One who was quieter than before. At least with me. I saw how she put on a face for others. Like she was squeezing into something too small, trying to shove down parts of herself she didn't want others to see. I couldn't fix any of it, and I didn't know how to make her feel better. All I did was worry. Aside from Khalil, I didn't know anyone who had died. I couldn't know what she was feeling, could only guess at that sort of grief, but I hoped this trip would at least serve as a temporary distraction. It was part of the reason I pushed so hard for us to be here. But *here*, wherever here was, wasn't exactly the plan.

"Tow truck will be here soon," she said when she heard me sit back down.

"Thanks for making the call."

She squeezed my hand in response, and my heart fluttered, just the tiniest bit. I was a little in love with Mira Hamdi. Not that Mira—or anyone, for that matter—knew. I was a little in love with the way she always took control of the situation. Whenever I thought of myself as the calm, cool-under-pressure one, she swooped in and saved the

day. Like when I twisted my ankle in gym last semester or when I forgot my film camera in her car over one hot summer weekend. Both times, Mira quickly quelled the tide of panic that threatened to flood over. I was a little in love with the way she laughed at the punch line of every joke I made before I made it because she knew exactly what I was thinking. God, I loved her laugh. I loved making her laugh. What a fleeting high it was to hear it.

I was a little in love with how her soft skin felt beneath mine right now. But Mira didn't know any of that, so I pulled away and sat up, looking for a tow truck heading toward us.

THREE

Mira

"The motel's just down this little gravel road. Can't miss it," the driver said as the tow truck slowed to a stop.

"Can you drive us the rest of the way though?" Layla asked. She looked confused in the dim overhead light.

"I would rather not" was all the man said. "Good luck."

"Thanks," I said, though it came out as more of a question. I pulled open the door handle and jumped outside. When I offered a hand to Layla, she jumped down on her own, holding the hem of her wet pale-green dress as she leapt. We took our bags from the cab of his truck. A red backpack and brown leather duffel for me, a camera bag and a small yellow rolling suitcase for her.

"It's a small town," the tow truck driver leaned forward to say. "Most of it within walking distance. Come by the garage tomorrow and Bill, the mechanic, will let you know the damage. Good night, ladies." He smiled reassuringly and drove off.

"Ready?"

Layla nodded, and we headed down the road. She seemed quiet, a little lost in thought as we fell out of step. Which felt odd, considering Layla always had something to say. Her long dark hair fell in soft waves, covering her face. She tucked one side behind her ear, still damp from the rain. I could see she was concentrating, focused on pulling her rolling suitcase along. She was only shorter than me by a few inches, but I wanted to wrap her in a bear hug and tell her that the car would be fine tomorrow morning, that we would make it to the portfolio day in Chicago in time, that the admissions department would love her photos and admit her on the spot, standard procedure be damned. But we both knew we weren't going to make it in time, so there was no use lying to her.

Finally, we saw the motel. A long one-level building that had seen better days. An orange neon sign that read WILDWOOD MOTEL hummed above the center, which was a story higher than the rest. Beneath it, two signs that read OFFICE and VACANCY flickered. I led us toward the signs but slowed down to let Layla catch up. Her suitcase really wasn't built for gravel.

"Almost. There," she said through gritted teeth. She paused and took a deep breath. "You know what? Go on without me. I'll catch up in a minute."

"You sure?"

She sat down on top of her suitcase and nodded, stretching both legs out in front of her. Nothing would move Layla now.

I stepped inside and pushed the door open with my back, heaving my duffel bag toward the foot of the front desk with both hands.

"Hi," I said to the two people behind it. It seemed like I had interrupted their conversation, but they both chuckled, amused by my graceful entrance, I'm sure.

"I got this, Izzy," the boy sitting on the high-top chair said as he adjusted his round glasses. "You can go help my mom if you want."

She looked like she was in her early twenties. Black linework tattoos adorned her left arm. I marveled at them for a second, studying the way they flowed in and out of one another as they melted into her brown skin.

She narrowed her eyes at him and nodded. "Mm-hmm, sure I can. I'll be in the back if you need anything," she told him, and left.

"How can I help you?" he asked as he moved his open book aside.

"I would love a room for me and my friend."

"No problem." He turned to his computer and began typing. My eyes lit up when I noticed his T-shirt.

"I love Alabama Shakes."

He looked up at me, confused, but smiled and said, "Me too."

I gestured at his band T-shirt until he finally connected the dots.

"Oh." He smiled. "That makes more sense than you randomly sharing that information."

"I have the same T-shirt. Got it when I saw them live in Detroit. We should have coordinated."

"If only we hadn't met thirty seconds ago!" He threw his hands up in fake anger and laughed. He had a nice laugh. Soft and full.

Just then, Layla opened the office door and kicked her suitcase inside, where it landed on its back. She gently removed her camera bag from her right shoulder and set it on top.

The boy watched with wide eyes. He stood up, wondering if he should help, but Layla looked angry, and I didn't blame him for reconsidering. She nodded at him, her lips in a tight line.

"What name should I put this under?"

"Mira Hamdi." He glanced at me then, just for a second, as if consciously committing face and name to memory.

"Where are you guys coming from?"

"Ann Arbor, Michigan, I guess." Technically, the last

city we were in was Nashville, but I figured he was asking us where we were from.

"One night?" he asked, turning back to the computer.

Layla and I looked at each other. Ideally, sure, we'd be back on the road by tomorrow. But we'd both seen the car. This seemed unlikely.

"For now? Our car broke down, and we're here until it's fixed."

"Oof, that sucks," he said. He wove his hand through his hair to keep it at bay and focused on the screen. He seemed to be our age, give or take. He was lean, about my height. White, with dark, expressive eyebrows that were knitted together. I couldn't help but notice the sharp line of his jaw and the way his deep brown eyes squinted at something he saw. The boy looked up, studying us. It looked like he was trying to make up his mind about something.

"I'm really sorry, but we're actually booked. There's a bed-and-breakfast in town. You might have better luck there," he said, his voice low.

Layla sighed behind me, clearly already dreading the walk into town with her suitcase.

"Thanks anyway," I said. I wondered if they'd mind us lying down in their parking lot for the night. I wasn't sure either of us would make it into town at this point. As we turned to leave, a woman emerged from the back room, a warm smile spread across her face.

"Ellis, honey, check again. These young ladies shouldn't have to trek all the way to Janet's place this late. I'm sure we have something available."

"Mom, there's nothing," he told her. They stared at each other until his mom finally broke the silence.

"Check again," she said, her smile a little forced now. Finally, he glanced back at the computer.

"Looks like Room 9 is open. Two keys?"

"Yes?" I said. Layla looked at me, confused. *You and me both, girl.*

"Here you go. Will that be cash or card?" He was avoiding eye contact now, busying himself with something on his screen. I handed over my emergency credit card. If this wasn't the time to use it, I didn't know what was. He slid it through the card reader and quickly handed it back.

"Please enjoy your stay."

He placed two keys on the counter and stood, walking past his mom and up the stairs on the back wall. She smiled at us and straightened the pamphlets on the desk.

"There's a conference in the city this week, so it's been very busy around here. And with another booking earlier today and now Room 9, we're fully booked," the mom said with a grin. She couldn't hide her excitement.

"That's great. Glad we can be the final guests," I said.

"I'm Elena, by the way. Shout if you need anything."

"Will do. Have a good night," Layla said pointedly, ready to end the conversation.

We gathered our things and headed toward the room, counting down the numbers along the right side of the building. I turned to make sure Layla was behind me and found her a few feet away, looking through her viewfinder. She clicked, and the sound of the shutter seemed louder in the quiet.

The second we were inside, Layla walked toward one of the beds, the one closest to the bathroom, and threw herself on top, shedding her bags and jacket as she went.

"Tired already?" I asked, smiling. She mumbled something into the mattress but made no effort to move. Objectively, the room wasn't as bad as I thought it would be. Two sets of sheer and beige blackout curtains lined the window behind me, the dark red carpet hid any stains it most likely held, and a small TV sat opposite the two twin beds. But it also felt—well, I'm not sure what it felt like, just that I felt heavy in it, weighed down by something outside of me. The room felt small, the air thin. My heart sped up, as if preparing me for something I couldn't see.

"I'm going to get some fresh air," I said. She gave me a thumbs-up from her bed and let her arm drop with a soft thud.

The spring air felt good in my lungs, cool and brisk. I could swear it was different here, fuller. There wasn't much

to do but wander, and so I found myself turning the corner of the motel. In the distance I could see a pool glistening, blue and bright from the lights beneath the surface. My lungs suddenly felt tighter, like the April air had seeped out of them without my noticing. I fought it back and headed toward the pool. The lounge chair was damp from the rain, and so I laid out my leather jacket and sat on top, near the edge, keeping a safe distance from the water. Almost a year later and I still couldn't look at a pool—or lake or ocean or any body of water, really—without having to remind myself to breathe.

I twisted in the chair and kept my back to the pool. No use in dredging up memories best kept buried. No, there were other things to focus on. Like how my parents would see the motel charge on their credit card and wonder why we were here. It was off the preapproved itinerary, and though I doubted they would care too much, it was best to avoid the possible situation entirely. I took out my phone and pulled up the group chat with my parents.

Car broke down in Wildwood, Indiana. Staying in town until the car is fixed. We're okay.

I clicked send and put my phone away. I imagined my mom seeing the text in the morning, once her nightly dose of sleeping pills had worn off, of course. She'd glance at it, maybe toy with the idea of calling to see if I was okay, but would ultimately abandon that thought to spend a few more hours refusing to leave her bed. I could count the times she'd left her room in the past year on one hand. My dad, on the other hand, had abandoned the idea of sleep entirely. When I asked why he was always up, he said, "Felt like we needed some balance around here." He said it jokingly, smiling, but the smile never reached his eyes, and he was quiet after that.

It had been quiet at home for a long time now, and if I was being honest, it was part of the reason I'd jumped at the chance when Layla suggested this trip. Anything was worth taking a week away from that stifling silence. From walking past Khalil's closed door or sharing a bathroom with nothing but his absence. A year later and none of us had the heart to throw out his toothbrush. Maybe I was running from his memory, but I was good at running.

This entire trip was planned around our college acceptances and Layla's one waitlist. I was most likely choosing the University of Chicago after a campus tour a few months ago. Seeing the other stops was just necessary confirmation of what I already knew. Sure, my major was undecided at the moment, but that campus, the city, it just felt right. Plus, leaving home was a necessity at this point. I didn't know how much longer I could stand living under the same roof as two parents who sat so deep in their own grief that they left no room for anything else. Layla, though, didn't have that same certainty. Her parents expected her to stay close to home at the University of Michigan, where the in-state tuition was reasonable. Her acceptance had hung on the fridge since the day it arrived. She hadn't even told them about her scholarship to Parsons School of Design in New York. *Why start a fight over something I haven't even made a decision on?* she'd said. Once we came back from the trip, she promised, she would tell them. If she decided on leaving, that is. My parents, on the other hand, had abandoned me. I could have told them I was going on this trip by leaving them a vague note: *Off to the see the world. Be back soon!* And they might not have thought twice about it. I almost wished I had, just to see what they would've done.

We had left Ann Arbor six days ago and begun a nine-hour drive to New York City. The next day, we toured Parsons and visited NYU's scattered buildings through Greenwich Village. We ended it with a chilly picnic at Washington Square Park before we started the short drive to DC. Georgetown felt like it had always existed. Like the rest of the city was merely built around it. Then came Nashville, which was everything DC wasn't, loud and vibrant.

We spent our one night there listening to a band we hadn't heard before and dancing until our legs begged us to go back to the hotel. After a day, we looped around and started heading toward Chicago, before ending up here, in good old Wildwood, Indiana. Not exactly the detour we had in mind, but things could be worse.

It was getting late, and tomorrow would most likely be a long day. I grabbed my jacket and was heading back toward the room when I saw the front desk boy, Ellis, making his way toward the pool. I waved when we were close enough, but he seemed to hesitate before saying good night.

"Night," I said, and kept walking. Odd, but the night's events were finally catching up with me, and the only thing I had mental space for was sleep.

I gently closed the door behind me. The room was dark except for a single lamp between the two beds and a smaller motel sign that shone through the window. Layla was fast asleep. At least she had changed into her pajamas and made it under the covers. Her hair fanned out around her pillow, dark as night around her brown skin. I got changed, climbed into bed, and turned off the lamp that she must have kept on for me.

But in the sudden darkness, I saw a silhouette of a man standing in the middle of the parking lot, the shape of him made of the orange neon light that fell down from the sign above. I couldn't tell if he was watching us or was turned away, but as far as he was, I could feel his gaze like a tangible thing. It was a third person in the room, bigger than either of us. Every part of me ached to reach over and pull the curtains closed. But instead I lay there, still as he was.

FOUR

The girl stares at the parted curtains, afraid to blink. A figure stands in the middle of the parking lot, unmoving. She can swear the figure, tall and broad shouldered, is facing them, watching her and her friend, but it is dark, and the only light that comes through is from the motel sign that glows bright and orange in the night. All she can make out is his silhouette and the light that surrounds him, like the edges of him are burning. She does not understand why his innocuous presence unnerves her, just that it does. Finally, after one long minute, the man walks away. The girl, broken from her spell, quickly pulls the curtains closed and lies back down. The girl twists in bed, trying to find sleep, to tuck the memory of him away. Eventually, she drifts.

Here is where the fun begins.

The girl tumbles into sleep. Messy and restless, but eventually the dream forms. The Pull begins. People tend to hide things, even from themselves. Feelings, memories. Other people. They keep them in their darkest corners, and when a light shines through, these demons have no choice but to come clambering out.

The dream begins in darkness. True darkness. The kind that makes you doubt if your body has ever existed. Have you always been a voice suspended in nothing? Little by little, pieces take shape.

The water is first. It is sudden and it is everywhere. There is no up or down, no direction. The Pull goes deeper, tugging at a particularly restless thought. Slowly, that too forms. A shape surrounds the girl inside the water. First limbs and torso, then a face that is too blurry to make out. The girl fights to keep it at bay. She does not want to see this. Not yet. The limbs tighten around her. The arms push against her head. It sends her deeper into murky waters. The girl's lungs are burning.

She wakes with a start. The girl holds her hands to her chest and takes deep breaths. Her lungs can't seem to fill with enough air. She stays that way for a few seconds, sucking in as much as her body will allow. She can't seem to slow down her racing pulse.

Eventually, she makes her way to her friend's bed and folds herself next to her. The friend mumbles in sleep and shifts over, making room for the girl. Their bodies are puzzle pieces. Her pulse slows down, but she can't shake the dream or the feelings it has stirred up. She can sense something beneath her surface, clawing to get out.

WEDNESDAY

FIVE

Layla

Mira had her arm around my waist. I repeat. Mira had her arm around my waist. I didn't know what unlikely miracle had happened last night, but I was thankful for it. She was still asleep, her breathing soft and steady, but she had her arm draped over my side, and the heat of it could set me on fire. Slowly, I turned over and looked at her. Her olive skin seemed to glow where the streaks of sunlight landed.

Sometimes, it was nice to pretend we were more than we were. Obviously, I knew she loved me. We were best friends. That was a prerequisite to best friendship, but I wanted more. I wanted to tuck a loose caramel curl behind her ear. To brush my thumb against her soft cheek and glide it down to the scar at the edge of her jaw from a bike ride gone wrong when she was twelve. I wanted to kiss her awake. For her to kiss me back. Was I being greedy? Probably. Instead, I lay in that early morning light for a minute and pretended, letting myself think *friends* was only the beginning for us.

Being here, surrounded by the quiet of this small town and the early morning light peeking through the crack in the curtains, it felt different. We felt different. Like there was static in the air. As if the knowledge that there was no large city to distract us, no itinerary to check off, allowed us to be just us, whatever that meant. Or maybe it was all in my head. Maybe this charged quiet was of my own making. Eventually, I pulled away, gently shifting the blanket away from my side of the bed. My suitcase was open on the floor from when I'd grabbed pajamas last night. Near the top was a coral dress with a deep, wide V neckline and cloth buttons all the way down. I couldn't wear it back home without one of my parents demanding I go back to my room and change into something less haram. Here, though, no one could say shit. Ha.

I buttoned up the dress, grabbed my keys and wallet, and quietly slipped away in search of food, letting the door softly click behind me.

We had skipped dinner last night. The only option I could think of that didn't include hiking all the way to town was the vending machine. I scanned the options. Limited. But aha! Near the bottom, abandoned and most likely expired, were small glass bottles of orange juice. I pushed E7 and collected our drinks, wondering if the front desk had breakfast options. I wasn't sure what to expect in a place like this, but I felt hopeful. Yesterday may have been a shit show, but there was no reason today had to be too.

"Morning," the front desk boy said when I walked in. I nodded at him and turned to spot the pastries behind me. A box of half a dozen cinnamon buns rested on the dark wooden table, the frosting still soft and oozing down the sides.

"Perfect timing. They're still warm," he said.

"It was either this or nothing, so thanks," I said, smiling. I turned to leave, but then he stopped me.

"I'm Ellis, by the way. In case you or—Mira, right?— need anything."

My smile felt forced now, like my face was frozen in this half grimace. Of course this was about Mira. I didn't blame him, but come on, man. Keep it professional.

"I'm Layla, and we're good."

"Cool," he said. We stared at each other for a long second, neither knowing if that was the end of the conversation. I was ready to walk out by then, but he opened his mouth and quickly closed it. After another second of this, I needed to leave. This was getting weird.

"Did you guys sleep okay?" he asked.

"Yeah?" I didn't understand why he was trying to make conversation.

"I'm going to go now, before these get cold. Thanks again," I said. And with that I took my cinnamon buns and left.

By the time I made it back to the room, Mira was up. If scrolling in my bed was up.

"I have brought us a feast. No need to thank me. Sharing this spread of culinary delicacies with you is enough."

Her stomach growled at the sight of cinnamon buns.

"Oh my God, yes."

I handed her one and sat down across from her. We ate in silence for a minute, enjoying the sunlight that slipped past the curtains.

"I think the front desk boy asked about you, in a roundabout way," I said between bites. It wasn't surprising. A lot of people couldn't help but be enthralled by Mira. She had this effortless way of carrying herself, like there was a gentle force inside her and all you wanted was to be pulled in by it.

"Ellis?" she said, smiling. "He's kind of cute, right?"

"I guess? I don't know. He seems weird. Off. He asked how we slept. It felt creepy." And I meant it, but I also couldn't help the sting I felt knowing that maybe she was interested back. Mira had never been shy about dating. But I didn't need Ellis to be on the roster. This trip was about us. More than anything, I wanted it to stay that way.

"Maybe he was just being nice?" she said. "This place is weird, not him. I doubt many people sleep well here," she added, looking around. She seemed tense, like she was convinced something was watching her.

"I don't see it. Sure, I always thought motels would be gross, but this place is sort of charming. Has this vintage vibe I'm kind of dying to capture on camera. Look at this old floral wallpaper. What is that? Marigolds?" I said, studying the wall. "The green bathroom? This TV from at least four decades ago? It's nostalgic. Like it's frozen in time or something."

Mira looked confused, her drink stopping halfway to her mouth. "I don't feel that" was all she said. I noticed that the skin beneath her eyes was dark and thin. I thought she had stopped having the nightmares months ago, but maybe not.

"Did you have a bad dream last night?"

She licked the last of the icing off her thumb and kept her eyes focused on the orange juice. The glass clinked against her silver thumb ring. My matching ring rested around my pointer finger. She nodded, only slightly, and brought the OJ to her lips.

"Was it about Khal—"

"I think I'm going to go for a run. Thanks for breakfast, Layla." She stood up and began rummaging through her duffel between the two beds.

"Wait, Mira. You sure you don't want to talk about anyth—"

"I'm fine. Don't worry about me." She pulled out a T-shirt and sweatpants and left to change in the bathroom. She'd changed in front of me a million times, but I guess anything to avoid talking about her dream. She walked out of the bathroom and grabbed her phone. Curls had escaped her quick ponytail and rested on her back. I wanted to pry her feelings out of her, but I knew better than to push Mira. At least on this. She seemed different this morning, quieter. I could feel the distance she was creating between us. I didn't want to add to it.

She reached for the door and paused.

"Do you hear that?" she said.

I stopped chewing and listened. "No? What is it?"

"I—I don't know. It sounds like, like waves? It sounds like the ocean." She looked paler than she did a few seconds ago. Her eyes darted around the room, trying to find the source, but I still didn't hear anything.

"You okay, Mira?"

"I'm fine. I'll see you later." She put on her headphones and shoved the keys into her pocket, slamming the door behind her.

SIX

Mira

I focused on my breathing.

In.

Out.

Felt my lungs fill and release with every step I took. I began a loop around the motel, but when that only took a few minutes, I headed into town to check up on Keira. I had gotten that beautiful rusty 2004 Chrysler Sebring earlier this year. Sure, my parents had only bought the car for me so they didn't have to drive me anywhere, so that my mom could hole up in her room uninterrupted. But still. Keira was my most prized possession, and she was in pieces. Obviously, Layla and I were both okay, and that's what mattered most. But Keira. Keira mattered too.

The cut on the edge of my hairline still felt raw. I could feel it throbbing as I pushed myself forward. I touched it, but it wasn't bleeding, just there. The farther I was from the motel, the easier it was to breathe. I didn't understand how

Layla felt completely fine at the motel. She didn't feel how the air was heavier there, like the shadows hid something darker than themselves.

It was like we had slept in two separate rooms. And it wasn't just the figure in the parking lot, whatever that was. Objectively, I knew that wasn't all that odd. It just felt wrong. She may have been asleep for that, but I couldn't deny the weight of that room from the moment I first stepped into it. And maybe I couldn't blame the room for my dream—if anything, that must have been the pool, being too close to water. But it'd been months since I'd had drowning nightmares. I couldn't sleep for weeks after Khalil died, couldn't go anywhere without seeing him in a stranger's gait or every time I looked in the mirror. His curly hair the same as mine, only darker. Fourteen was too fucking soon.

The night before that trip to Tunisia, I had wandered into his room and thrown myself onto his unmade bed. He whipped around, then proceeded to ignore me, continuing to fill his suitcase with unfolded T-shirts like I wasn't there.

"We leave in the morning. You told Mom you packed," I said.

"Is it lying if I end up doing it eventually?" He tapped his temple, proud of his own logic.

"Are you excited?" I asked him. It had been five years since the last trip back. Khalil was only nine then. I was twelve.

He paused to think about the question. "A little bit. Mostly looking forward to spending two months reading on the beach. You?"

"Yeah, not looking forward to that initial awkwardness with everyone though. You know, they'll ask a million questions. *Tell us about America! Why are you so quiet? Why isn't your Arabic better? Do you like Tunis or America more?* Until they run out of things to say and we all have to wallow in the silence together."

He continued throwing clothes in, rearranging them just so.

"Do you miss it at all?"

He shrugged. "I don't know. We've been back there, what, three times? Hard to miss a place you can't remember." He lay back on a pile of clothes that I hoped were clean.

"The summer will go by fast. You'll be back here starting your sophomore year in no time."

"The key is to stay busy," he said with a smirk. And then he moved the top layer of clothes in his suitcase to reveal at least twenty books that he had packed for the summer.

"Oh my God, Khalil. If Mom doesn't figure it out when the airport charges us an overweight fee, she'll figure it out when you end up wearing the same three T-shirts for two months."

"Ah, but by then, there'll be nothing she can do." He smiled wide, the gap between his two front teeth showing, and I knew I couldn't tell him otherwise. I was going to need his traveling library.

Now I missed him like I missed a part of myself. It hurt to think of him, but it was also soothing in this uncomfortable, masochistic way. I'd lost a piece of me that day too, and here was a faint reminder of it.

No. No, this wouldn't do me any good. I needed him out. I pumped my legs harder. I took deeper breaths, feeling my lungs expand. I opened my eyes and focused on my surroundings. I was on the quiet tree-lined path that led away from the motel and into town. It looked different in the daytime. Eerier, somehow. The light came through the trees in scattered rays along the road, and logically, I knew it was beautiful. But it was also strange. The quiet permeated everything. There were no birds. No cars. And though I could see the town from a distance, I couldn't hear anything but my sneakers slamming against the pavement again and again, my rhythmic and heavy breathing matching my stride.

With my eyes focused on my running feet, I didn't notice the man coming around the corner until it was too late. My shoulder bumped into his and he stumbled for a second, righting himself—but not before his headphones were pulled out of his ears and onto the ground, along with his phone, the screen facedown.

"Shit, I'm so sorry!" I said, pulling out my own head-phones. He picked up his phone and slowly examined it. When he finally flipped it over, I could see that the screen was cracked, a fissure running across the pretty dark-haired woman on his background. He rubbed at the fractured glass, as if trying to brush it away from her face, to no avail. Shards of glass at the edge of the phone came off. "Oh no. That's totally my fault," I said. "I should have been paying attention."

"No, it's all right. It still works. See?" He slid his thumb against the screen to show me it was still responsive. "My fault for not putting a case on it, I guess." He put the phone in his pocket and held his hand out for me to shake.

"I'm Devlin, by the way."

"Mira." Both of our hands were sweaty from running, but we laughed and wiped them on our shirts. Even with a full dark beard lining his jaw, I could see the dimples in his cheeks. He looked a little older, late twenties perhaps, and was easily six feet tall. His dark hair was matted down with sweat, glistening in the weak sunlight that made it past the trees.

"You're in Room 9, right?"

"Yeah?" How odd. He must have noticed the suspicion on my face, because he held his hands up.

"I saw you and your friend check in last night is all. Your friend looked like she was having trouble with her suitcase, but something about her face told me she'd only be angrier if I offered to help. I'm a few doors down, Room 7." He had the soft lilt of an Irish accent that had all but left him.

"Ah, okay. Yeah, that sounds like Layla."

I could hear the sound of tire tracks against gravel as a car tried to maneuver around us in the tight pathway behind me. We moved out of the way, flush against the trees, and when the car left, I took that as my cue too.

"I should get going. It was nice meeting you!" I said as I walked away.

He yelled out, "You too," but by then I was a few yards away, at the edge of the trees and the rest of town.

At the end of the road, Wildwood, Indiana, spread out before me. The tow truck driver hadn't been wrong. Even from here I could see that this road held everything a town needed. I kept running until I was close enough to read the store signs. The smell of fries and grease wafted out of Joan's Diner. There was an ice cream store called The Cone with a plastic scoop of pink-and-purple ice cream melting on a brown textured cone at the edge of the sign. A bowling alley named Gutter & Strike around the corner from it. A cute bookstore named Novel Tea was nestled between a pharmacy and a general store. A gas station was at the end of the road, and across from it was Bill's Garage.

The road that ran through all of it was wide and open,

quaint even. I had grown up in Ann Arbor, and sure, it wasn't the biggest city, but this felt miniature in comparison. A car came up behind me, and I jogged over to the sidewalk to get out of the way. Aside from a handful of people, it was empty. Though that could have been because it was Wednesday morning. People had things to do. I went inside the mechanic's shop and rang the bell on the desk. An older man sporting a backward baseball cap and overalls came out with a rag in his hands, trying to scrub away the black grease from his palms.

"How can I help you?"

"Hi, I'm Mira. Someone dropped off my car last night and said I should come back today to see how bad the damage is."

"Ah, yeah. The Chrysler Sebring. Looked like a pretty bad accident. What happened?"

I wasn't exactly eager to share that I swerved because I thought I saw someone standing in the middle of the road, especially when they disappeared soon after. "Must have been the rain. We skidded into the ditch."

"We've had a few accidents on that stretch of road. People have to be more careful. So, I'll be honest with you. It's not good," he said, wincing at having to say it.

I'd seen the car last night. This was not news. Still, having it confirmed hit like a sucker punch.

"How not good?"

"Well, your entire windshield is shattered from the air-bags deploying. You need new airbags. The glass on your right headlight is a goner too, as is that front axle and right rim," he said, counting them off with his grease-stained fingers. "It'll cost ya."

I closed my eyes for a second and put my hands against my face, wiping the sweat and strands of hair away. "Okay. That's fine. How long will it take?"

"I'll need a few days. Maybe Friday? We have most of the parts here, and I'll do my best to get you the rest sooner rather than later. You're staying at the motel, right?"

"Yeah."

"I'll overnight what I can, then. The sooner you're out of there, the better." He chuckled, but I didn't get the joke.

"Why? What do you mean?" Maybe it was the run, but I could feel my heart pound in my chest. There was something off about that place. Something wrong. I couldn't name it, but it was there. And here was someone who knew it too.

The man shook his head and busied himself with the pamphlets on the desk. I could see the dark smudges where his fingertips touched them.

"Come on, I love a good town legend," I said, smiling wide. Maybe I was laying it on thick, but the only answers I'd get from him were the ones I pulled out.

He hesitated for a moment, then set the grease-stained rag down on the wooden counter separating us and leaned closer, his voice low and serious now. "We've got a fine town here. Plenty of hardworking folks, a great community, and I stand by that. But things happen in that place. Strange things. Things people have a hard time explaining away, ya know?" He looked at me, as if expecting some sort of sign that I had grasped what he said.

I hadn't. "What strange things?"

"Trust me. The less you know, the better." He glanced behind me, as if making sure we were alone, and then continued. "I grew up in this town, spent my whole life here. Hell, I was here the first time it happened. None of us thought much of it then. But then it kept happening. And happening. People say it's haunted, and I reckon they're not too far off. You just can't have that much spilt blood without something staying behind. You understand?"

Understand? None of this was making sense. "What do you mean 'spilt blood'?"

"I'll get your car up and running in no time. Hang tight," he said instead of answering my question. He headed toward the door and waved, disappearing inside the garage.

I started my slow jog back, even more ready to get out of here than before. I didn't believe in *haunted*. Not usually, anyway. *Haunted* was for stories you told in the dark when the light wasn't there to prove you wrong. But something about the motel felt ominous. No, no. What was I thinking? I just needed to get out of my head. I needed a good night's sleep. I needed to stop thinking about my brother. I needed a healthy distraction that wasn't a fixation on things I couldn't change.

And yet. Layla.

Layla was in the room. I didn't like the idea of her alone there. I reached the gravel road that led to the motel and ran a little faster. The trees seemed to bend toward me, like the branches would tear at me if I ran too close to the edge. It felt harder to run toward the motel than away, like my legs were dipped in honey. Each step more difficult than the last. I needed a shower. I needed to wash this place off me before it had a chance of sticking.

Finally, the slightly crooked golden nine was in sight. But as I reached it, I could see through the wide window to the left of the door. Layla must have pulled the curtains open. Sunlight filtered in, bathing the room in muted warmth.

I looked closer, thinking it was a trick of the light at first, shadows playing against the sun, but no. There was someone there with his back to me. He sat on the edge of my bed, still, his head bowed. I was ready to run, to turn around, to go to the front desk or call someone, figure out how the hell someone had gotten into our room. But my eyes were fixed on the boy's bare shoulders. I recognized those shoulders, the freckles that were scattered there. I recognized that hair. His skin looked wet and gray.

My hands shook as I shoved the key into the lock. I didn't care if it was some stranger. I just needed to know one way or another. I opened the door, careful not to make any sudden movements. He didn't turn around. My head kept saying turn back. Run. Somewhere. Anywhere. It didn't matter. He may have had my brother's shoulders, the arc of his spine, but it didn't mean anything. I needed to see his face. I reached out toward his shoulder, my fingers trembling as they made contact with damp skin.

SEVEN

"Khalil?" she asks. Mira is afraid of what the answer will be. The boy begins to turn, but before she can see his face, he disappears, only wisps of gray smoke twisting in the air. Once again, she is alone in the room, but the shape of him is still apparent in the dusty sunlight that pours in. Her hand, suspended in midair, still shakes. She clenches it into a fist and releases. Her hands go to her head, swipe her loose strands of hair aside, and stay there. She does not know what she has just seen. Cannot make sense of it.

Mira looks around. Searches for any sign of him left behind. Something to prove his presence. There is nothing but her shadow laid out before her.

"I'm crazy. I'm going crazy," she mutters to herself, and looks back at the door, considers leaving. But minds are quick to try to make sense of the unexplainable. To create logic where there is none. And so she tells herself she's tired and most likely needs some sleep. That a shower will help. She makes her way into the bathroom and begins to undress. In the mirror, she thinks she can see something pressed against the translucent shower door, a hand maybe. She turns around, but there is nothing there. Slowly, she faces forward, and again she sees it in the mirror, a shape behind the glass. A shoulder pressed against it, the side of a head flush against the door. She doesn't look away this time. A part of her knows that nothing will be there when she checks.

Another part of her knows that this does not mean there is nothing there. She watches, her breath held tight in her chest, and waits. The figure squeezes a hand against his throat, stays there for too long, long enough that she needs to breathe by the time the figure slides down the door, the screech of skin against smooth glass echoing in the quiet bathroom. Slowly, a hand crawls up the glass, fingers light and steady, and reaches for the handle. The door edges open, and Mira whips around, her hands bracing the porcelain sink.

But of course, nothing is there. The shower door is shut tight, and there is no figure beyond the glass. No dead brother waiting for her. She feels both safe and terrified all at once. Mira rethinks the shower. Splashes some cold water on her face, dampens a towel and quickly slides it under her armpits and around her torso. Though there's nothing there, her eyes never leave the reflection of the shower door. Faster than ever before, she slides into a loose pair of pants the color of clay and belts them at the waist. She shoves her arms through an olive-green T-shirt. She grabs her phone, keys, the necessary cards from her wallet, stuffs them into her deep pockets. Mira glances around one last time and slams the door behind her.

EIGHT
Layla

I had my camera around my neck, trying to find something to capture. The sun was still high, casting everything
it touched into stark contrasts. My portfolio was severely
lacking in black-and-white photos, and I planned to spend
this trip correcting that. I'd even changed my settings to
shoot only in black and white instead of editing them later,
just so I couldn't wimp out. This way I didn't have the reassur-
ance that at least I got a good shot in color. No plan B
meant plan A better be good. I'd avoided it long enough.
No photo during this trip would be in color.

At this point though, I itched to abandon the plan. So
what if my black-and-white photos sucked? I didn't need
to know how to shoot every style. But I knew that was just
the avoidance talking. I needed to stay firm. By the end of
this, I'd have a collection of simple and dramatic photos
that cataloged Mira's and my entire trip. The few photos I
had taken of departing guests left something to be desired,

but I just needed to focus. To find the shot. The light. The story.

I framed the edge of the motel in half of the shot and watched as Mira walked into the other. She looked distracted, a little lost in thought. I clicked and checked the display, but something wasn't right. The edges of the building and ground bent around her, and though it was barely noticeable, it was impossible to unsee. Maybe my camera had taken a hit last night and I was only now realizing it. I shifted the camera to my side and waited for her to reach the pool chairs.

"Thought you might be here," she said.

"Because there's nowhere else to go?"

She half smiled, but something felt off. Her shoulders were tense, her neck taut. My hands itched to hold hers, or wrap her in my arms until she felt better about whatever was off, but I kept my hands folded in my lap.

"Everything okay?" I asked instead. She nodded and laid out on the pool chair. She closed her eyes and bent her face toward the sun. Was she avoiding looking at the water? I could see her chest rise and fall, like she was taking deeper breaths than she needed to. Slowly, she seemed to relax, and her shoulders eased their way down.

"Did you call your parents yet?" she asked, changing the subject before I had a chance to even bring it up. Her eyes were still closed.

I groaned at the thought of having to let them know about this particular predicament. They wouldn't react well. "I've been putting it off, but I guess I should get it over with."

"Let me know how it goes." She turned over in the pool chair to look at me. "I went into town, by the way. The mechanic said most likely Friday, in case they ask."

"I guess it could have been worse. It's, what? Wednesday today? We'll be fine. It's not so bad here."

"Still. I'm sorry we're missing the portfolio day."

I shrugged. "No use in wondering what could have been."

She looked like she wanted to say more, like she was searching my eyes for something, but whatever it was, she didn't find it. She smiled, small and tight, and turned back.

I stood up and pulled my phone out, tapping my dad's contact picture. I could call my mom, but I didn't have that in me just yet. At least my dad could be a little reasonable about this.

"Loulti, how are you?" he said in Arabic.

"I'm good, I'm good," I said, switching to Arabic. "I just wanted to tell you something."

"One second, your mom wants to say hi." *Well, there goes that plan.*

"Hi, Mom," I said. They turned on the video chat and

I had no choice but to reciprocate, forcing a smile. My dad had the camera close to his face, his salt-and-pepper beard taking up most of the screen. He looked down at the phone over the edge of his round brown glasses and finally moved the phone away so that I could better see them.

"Layla, let me see you," my mom said. "Are you eating? Have you been taking the vitamins I packed in your bag? You know how impo—"

"Yup, I have. Everything is fine. I'm fine," I said, interrupting.

"Wait, what is that behind you? Where are you right now?" Her smile quickly dropped. She looked concerned for moment, her green eyes wide and alarmed before they turned suspicious, her dark eyebrows knitting together. I started walking back toward the pool, but it was too late. She had seen the Wildwood Motel sign over my shoulder. Loud and clear. I didn't even get a chance to work up to it.

"That's actually what I called to talk about," I said. "Mira's car broke down outside of Wildwood, Indiana, so we got sidetracked from the itinerary. It just happened last night," I added. I decided to leave out the car accident. I had enough to deal with. I didn't need to freak them out more than I already had. For a second, it looked like the connection had cut off. Both of their faces were frozen. But then they spoke up at the same time. *Are you okay? Where is*

Wildwood? Why wouldn't you tell us as soon as it happened? You have to come back now. We'll come pick you up. The questions and demands overlapped so much I couldn't tell who was asking what. But it didn't matter. God no. I'd rather be in this motel for the rest of the trip than cut it short to be picked up by my parents.

"I knew this was a bad idea. You're both seventeen," my mom said, as if I didn't know. If they could have it their way, one to four parents would have made this trip with us. Arab parents took overprotectiveness to new, almost impressive, levels. But neither of my parents could take off work for the times we needed them to, and Mira's parents weren't really an option. I had been surprised when my parents said yes, even if their yes had included a hundred conditions. I *still* was. But Mira's parents asked a few questions and handed over the emergency credit card. They didn't even offer to come.

My mom turned to my dad. "We shouldn't have let her do this. Out in God knows where. No car. No food. Illegal drugs and dangerous men everywhere." I wanted to laugh. Mira and I had spent the previous week in several of America's major cities. NYC, DC, Nashville. Chicago would have been one of them too if it weren't for last night. But one tiny town off the preapproved itinerary and my mom was ready to ship me back.

"Mom, calm down. It's safe. It's clean. And it's only for a day or two. I have yet to see a single drug, and there's, like, one boy who works the front desk. It's practically boring. I promise."

"This is just another sign! You better be getting this whole trip out of your system. Once you're home, no more talk of out-of-state college or your photography thing. Just because Mira's parents don't care what happens to her doesn't mean you can do whatever you want too." She paused for a moment, mostly to take a breath, and continued. "Have your fun now, but when you come back, it's time to be serious."

I had to put all my energy into relaxing my jaw, into not lashing out. It wasn't time. It wouldn't have done anything. I had told them this trip was for Mira, that I was only tagging along while she looked at colleges. We had already heard back from the schools we applied to, but why not see the places we wanted to go to before we had to make any decisions. They didn't know about my scholarship to Parsons or me getting waitlisted at SAIC. Or the handful of other schools I had gotten accepted to that were all very, very far from Michigan. They assumed I'd already agreed to go somewhere near home even though I had never said it. I just hadn't had the guts to tell them otherwise. Sure, they suspected that I had my eyes on these schools too.

Especially after my mom had found the college pamphlets in my room. I thought I was being clever by having them mailed to Mira's house first, but my mom found them within days of me picking them up. I should have known. Nothing stays a secret for long in the Saleh house.

My father had receded to the background. He knew there was no way he was going to get a word in edgewise, and I'm sure it seemed like my mom had a handle on the situation. "I want you in your motel room the whole time. And no need to be talking to that boy. Just because you're in a different state doesn't mean the rules are any different." It took all of me not to roll my eyes at the camera. I nodded, but she kept pushing.

"Do you understand?"

"Yes, yes. I heard you." I looked at Mira splayed out on the pool chair, her long legs in terra-cotta pants tied at the waist, the delicate curve of her neck angled upward. She had her eyes closed, her head tipped toward the sun. She shifted, and a sliver of skin peeked through her crop top. Boys had never been an issue. No one knew how I felt about Mira, least of all my parents. I barely understood it, what it meant, what it made me. But the second I started to consider telling them about whatever it was I was feeling, things would change. They were good people. I loved my parents. They loved me. But their love wasn't unconditional, no matter how much they wanted it to be.

Mira had come out to me as bi last year. But that didn't mean I had the green light to throw myself into her arms. If Mira didn't feel the same way, I would lose her. And if I told my parents, I would lose them. Why risk tearing everything apart? At least this way, I could still keep them all in my life and the only person miserable, confused, and uselessly pining would be me. What a plan.

"I'm going to go. I think Mira's calling me. I'll talk to you guys later." My mom gave me a tight smile and said goodbye. My dad waved from the back, though I could tell he wanted to say more. I ended the call, but a few seconds later, my phone buzzed with a text from my dad.

We're glad you two are okay. Let us know if you need anything. See you soon.

The *we* was presumed, I'm sure, but it was still sweet. Sometimes I wondered what it would be like to have a better relationship with my mom. A healthier one that didn't leave me frustrated after most conversations. But that wasn't us and maybe it never would be. Maybe expecting the impossible from each other was only setting us up to fail. I sent a heart back and took a deep breath. Bright side. I needed to look on the bright side. A few days off schedule could be great. Maybe this could be an adventure. I wasn't sure what Wildwood had to offer, but if there was anything, we would find it. And this place wasn't bad. It was sort of beautiful. Ahead of me was a tree-lined trail that led to the road, its shadows making patterns across the dirt path. I definitely needed a shot of that later. The grass was a little yellow, but that just added character. Who doesn't love character? Yeah, this would be fine. I made my way back to Mira and plopped down on the chair next to her.

"How are Mama and Baba Saleh?" Mira said. We didn't really speak Arabic together. There were as many dialects as there were Arabic-speaking countries, and our two were just different enough that English felt easier, but it was always nice to hear the correct pronunciation of the words we shared.

"They freaked out, as expected, but they'll get over it. Considering they're not driving down here to pick us up and cut this trip short, I'd say it was a successful call."

She smiled but didn't say anything.

"So, what should we do today?" I asked.

"I think I saw someone, something, in our room," she said at the same time.

"What? There was someone in our room? Like someone was in there to clean it?"

She shook her head. I waited for her to say more, but she looked like she had to pull it out of herself.

"I don't know. Someone was sitting on the bed and then

they weren't. After, I went into the bathroom to shower, but there was something behind the glass door. The shape of someone. I thought—" She paused. "I thought it was my brother."

"What do you mean? Was someone there?" The idea of someone sneaking into our room made my skin crawl.

"I—I don't know. I don't think so. He just disappeared. Like I had imagined him or something?"

"Oh, Mira." My heart ached at her words. I knew she missed her brother. It hadn't even been a year yet. But she had also taken a hard hit to the head yesterday. Were hallucinations a symptom of concussions? "Are you sure? Maybe we should have gone to the hospital after the accident. You could have hit your head pretty hard." I leaned toward her, my hand reaching for the cut on the edge of her forehead, before I realized what I was doing. She flinched and sat up.

"I'm fine. Forget it. It's nothing. I haven't slept well, that's all," she said. "Why don't we go into town and find something to do? I saw a bowling alley. I know how much you love those," she joked, changing the subject.

I fake vomited, sticking my tongue all the way out. "How is wearing the same pair of shoes a thousand people already wore and sweated in a thing we decided was okay?"

"You only hate it because you're bad at it," she said.

"Yeah, well, that doesn't help."

"Okay, okay. But there is a bookstore I want to check out."

"You should have led with that. Let me just get my stuff from the room."

She looked at me for a long moment, suddenly serious, like she was searching my face for something that wasn't there. She nodded.

I grabbed my camera and went back to the room. A part of me was waiting for someone to slither out from under the bed, but it was only an empty room. Worn but warm and welcoming. Mira was grieving. I saw the way she stood by the pool, wary of its edges. I wanted to help, but I was at a loss for words or actions. All I could do was be there, whether she found my presence comforting or not. What I did know was that if it were me dealing with everything she was going through, Mira would be my only reprieve.

I quickly checked my reflection in the bathroom mirror. Over my shoulder was the shower door. It was translucent and unassuming, and yet, I couldn't resist sliding it open. It was like Schrödinger's cat was inside and until I checked for myself, Mira and I were both right. Of course, there was nothing there. It was silly to have checked at all.

I grabbed my camera bag, made sure my wallet and keys were in there, and headed toward the door before I remembered the weird warping in my last photo. Before Mira had come, I had taken a few photos of departing guests, but those photos seemed fine. None of them had me second-guessing my lens or settings knowledge. I went back to the bathroom and took a photo of myself. Mostly out of curiosity. But the photo looked like it should.

I went back to the pool chairs expecting to find Mira still lazing in the sun, but she wasn't there anymore. She wasn't in the parking lot either, and as much as I didn't want to be right, I went to the office front desk and there she was, smiling into a conversation with Ellis.

"You ready?" I asked.

"Yeah," Mira said. She turned to me with one eyebrow raised, her head slightly cocked to the right toward Ellis, and bit her lip. I knew what she was trying to tell me. I did not like it. *No*, my eyes screamed back. But it wasn't coming across like I needed it to, because she turned back to him and said, "We're heading into town for what will undoubtedly be food. Do you want to come?"

He paused for a second, his eyes focused on Mira.

"You'll need a tour guide to see everything the sprawling metropolis of Wildwood has to offer. Give me five minutes to wrap up here and tell my mom?"

"Sure thing," Mira said, laughing. It wasn't even funny. I kept my eye roll to myself and pulled open the door. Mira

followed and we went outside to wait for him. It was just like her to invite him, impulsive and rash.

"We could have figured it out on our own. You didn't need to invite him," I said.

"I know. He just seemed nice. He's only a year younger than us, a junior. Also, did you see him reading Jandy Nelson? How often do we meet people who aren't lame? You guys are bound to get along."

"Whatever, just didn't need some stranger crashing our trip," I said. I kept my hands busy adjusting the buttons on my dress, avoiding her eyes. Why couldn't she see that I wanted her to slow down for once and think this through? We didn't need him.

"It's only an afternoon. We won't ever see him again in a day or two."

I shrugged. It was too frustrating to argue about. Especially when I couldn't tell her I hated the way she laughed at his jokes, like her whole face lit up.

Behind us, Ellis came out of the office. He wore a white T-shirt, orange detailing around the neckline and sleeves, that he tucked into a pair of jeans. The rip at the pocket looked like it was from time, not fashion. He jogged a few steps away to the vacancy sign to the left and flipped a switch. The NO flickered to light.

"There's a conference in a nearby city, if *city* is what you want to call it. We're booked for the week," he said.

"Your mom told us last night. She seemed psyched about it. That's awesome," Mira said.

"Yeah, I guess." He stared at the neon sign for a second and then finally turned back to us. "Okay, let's do this."

We began heading toward the path that led into town. I walked next to them but eventually let them walk a few steps ahead. When Mira turned back to ask why I was trailing behind, I raised my camera in response. Underneath that archway of green leaves and high branches, I wanted to be angry. But Mira and Ellis were a picture walking down the center. I framed the shot and clicked. They had their backs to me, but they were both perfect. Like they fit. The way they moved, they looked like they belonged, like they had known each other longer than these twelve hours.

I checked the display and found that the image had slight warping on one side, the corner and trees bending against their will. Maybe I needed to recalibrate the lens, but it was a whole process and I hadn't even brought what I needed to do that. I just had to settle for being frustrated with every photo, knowing I couldn't make them look like I knew they should. The camera strap tugged at my neck and I let it. I looked up at them. Mira's sun-kissed curls fell down her back. His cropped sides and wavy top framed his face well. She said something funny because Mira's funny, and he threw his head back and laughed.

I wanted to hear the joke, but I didn't feel like asking

her to repeat it. Mira had liked people before. She'd dated all through high school. In secret from her family, sure, but that never stopped her. I watched as she crushed over so many boys and girls that I could never nail down her type, especially this past year. Not that there was anything I could do with that information. Maybe it would have been nice to better predict her, but who was I kidding. This was Mira. She did what she wanted, like casually flirt with the front desk boy, and all I could do was watch while she did it.

I focused on Mira this time, lowering the camera so that it was angled upward. She turned back right before I clicked. The wind moved through her curls and quickly settled. Her eyes connected with mine instead of the lens, and everything around her fell away in a hazy bokeh blur. She didn't look away, even when I let go of the camera.

I looked down, partly to study the display and mostly to calm my quick heartbeat. It didn't matter how upset or annoyed I was with Mira—I couldn't not take a picture of her. It's like it was out of my control. There wasn't an angle that didn't do that girl justice. I reveled in the fact that this, here, felt familiar. At least with a camera between us, I could almost convince myself it was just us on this trip. It was Mira and Layla versus everyone else. But I half pressed the shutter button and the focus faltered for a second, reminding me that Ellis very much existed only a foot away.

I jogged between them, and Mira stepped back to let me get a shot of Ellis in the speckled light before I quickly walked ahead of them. Mira was used to me taking my camera everywhere, making her model for me every time I liked a streak of light or had an idea. But Ellis surprisingly rolled with it, following Mira's lead. He turned to me and posed, giving me his most serious model face, half bathed in shadow. At least he made for good photos. They laughed and it was impossible not to notice how close their hands were. I clicked, perhaps a little too hard this time, and let my camera rest at my hip. I had memorialized enough of this walk.

NINE

Mira

Ellis took us to the bookstore first, a safe bet for three readers. He stood near the register for a moment, letting us take it all in. At the front were torn boxes filled with records and cassette tapes. An old and dusty piano sat near the window, the lid open and seat pulled out, an invitation to be played. But then the books. Dark wooden shelves lined the walls, and between them were aisles that were tight and overflowing with paperbacks and hardcovers, as if the owner had squeezed in one more aisle than they should have. In the center was an opening that many of the aisles fed into. The place was old and worn, like every single stack of books that was piled high on the floor had been chosen with the utmost care. I would bet anything that if I studied a pile closely, I could find some sort of theme tying them all together. Books with the most atmospheric fictional towns. Characters with the best comebacks. The owner's favorite villains.

Near the back was an entire wall devoted to children's

books. Everything from picture books to young adult. None of which were categorized in any intelligible way—at least not one I could make sense of. Ellis joined me and stood a few feet away, studying the wall intently. He took out a book with a red cover and opened it to read the inside jacket.

Layla wandered off down the aisles of used books, searching for treasure. I looked at her, trying to get her to look back, to make sure we were okay, but she avoided me, her fingertips dancing along the spines of old books. I knew bringing Ellis annoyed her, but he made for a good distraction, and Layla couldn't keep asking me what was wrong if he was tagging along. Logically, I knew she was right. How could there be anything in that room? I'd hit my head too hard last night, and if I was smart, I would have gone to get it checked. A quick Google search confirmed that hallucinations could be a symptom of concussions.

But what if.

What if the figure I'd seen before we crashed was connected? What if I could go back to that stretch of road and find something, anything, to make me feel not as crazy? But no. There would be nothing to find.

I pushed the thought away and focused on not letting her think that I was losing my mind. She looked delicate in her long-sleeve coral dress with the buttons all the way

down, her camera strapped against her body. She wandered toward the piano and sat down, setting her camera bag next to her. Her fingers froze for a moment, away from the keys, before they softly played a rising melody, stumbling once or twice as the song built. She stopped taking lessons years ago but the notes were still there, waiting for a piano to appear. I could see the dust suspended in the light, the sun silhouetting her profile. She looked like magic.

I took out my phone and snapped a shot, trying to frame the light just so and figuring I should center her. I clicked and her hands were poised over the keys, ready for the next note to come. But it was no use. I couldn't capture this. I couldn't capture her. Layla never got to be in the pictures, not really. She always took these gorgeously soft and warm photos of me. I felt bad I couldn't return the favor. I used to try, but after a while, I realized they weren't the same. There was something about the way she framed a shot, the way she found the opportunity in every mundane thing I didn't look twice at. She had an eye for it that I didn't. She'd tell me to stop, to pose, to move, and then everything would fall into place around me. I wondered if it was me she found, like she could see my shiny parts and knew how to make them shimmer against the light, if only she framed it just so. She glanced at me, saw the phone

in my hand, and quickly looked away. I couldn't tell if the blush that crept up her cheeks was imagined or not.

Sometimes, I wondered if Layla had feelings for me. There were moments where I was convinced. The way she would pause after I asked a question about boys or the moments I would catch her looking at me when she didn't think I was looking. Sometimes, I felt like Layla held some part of her so close to her chest that even I, who knew her best, would never know her fully. Could I blame her? There were things about *me* that she didn't know. Things I couldn't say out loud. I'd be a hypocrite to demand I know all of her.

"Have you read this?" Ellis asked. I tore my eyes away from Layla and looked at the book he held.

"No, not yet. But it's Angie Thomas, so can you really go wrong?" He studied the book for a second and looked at the inside jacket again. I could see his eyes go to the price.

"Actually, I'm going to buy this," I said, taking the book from his hands and quickly flipping through it. "Consider it a thank-you present for showing us around town." I closed the book and began to head toward the cash register.

"Whoa, wait. No, I can't accept that." He ran ahead and planted himself in front of me. He extended both arms out toward the shelves to block me. It was a narrow aisle, and both his hands reached the shelves easily. "If anything, you're doing me a favor by getting me out of the motel for an afternoon. So no present required."

"Even so, I'd feel a lot better if you didn't argue. So," I said. I could see him tense, ready to grab the book, but I raised it just out of reach. He lunged for it, but he wasn't that much taller than me, and it was a pretty fair fight.

"Nope! I'm doing it!" I yelled a little too loudly for a bookstore, then twisted around him and ran to the front. There were a few book piles stacked along the way, and I quickly maneuvered around them, a little proud that I hadn't knocked a single one down. Ellis finally caught up with me at the cash register but only after I handed my emergency credit card to the man behind the desk. What's one more charge? He had smiled when he saw the book. I liked to think that he had read every single book in here. Ellis was breathing a little hard, but he took the paper bag with the book from him.

"Thanks," he said, bumping my shoulder with his.

"You are very welcome. Now let's find Layla. I'm starting to get hungry."

I found her deep down one of the stacks and waved her over.

"Find anything?"

"It's an honor to be nominated," she said, cracking a smile. It was our little joke. It's nice just to be here. I don't

need an award, or in this case, a book, out of it. Ellis looked confused, but I had the sneaking suspicion that if I explained it, Layla would be upset again, so I let it sit there. We left the bookstore, the bell atop the door ringing behind us.

Out of the corner of my eye, I saw him.

Khalil.

His curly dark hair. His lanky frame. The awkward bow of his neck, like he was growing too fast for his body. My heart pounded at the sight of him. I froze in place, too afraid to take a step toward or away from him. But then the boy turned, and it wasn't Khalil at all. Just a kid heading toward the ice cream shop across the street, and I was just losing my mind. I didn't know what I'd seen back in the room. My mom would say it was a djinn, that I needed to read a surah from the Quran and cleanse the room by lighting some bkhour. I didn't believe in that. At least I didn't think I did, but I had no explanation for what I'd seen.

"Mira?" Ellis said.

"What?"

"I said do you guys want to go to the diner. The food is . . . fine. It's fine. I'm not going to lie to you guys. Just don't order anything with tuna. Please."

"Diner sounds great. Lead the way, Ellis," Layla said, answering for both of us. She was looking at me, concern in her eyes. I smiled at her reassuringly and followed Ellis a few buildings down. It was fine. I was stuck in my head. Clearly, I was having some sort of delayed response to my own grief. What I'd seen in the room, I had imagined. And now, with my mind firmly on it, I was adding details that weren't there. Like the taste of salt water on my tongue or the feel of sand beneath my fingernails. There was nothing there. My mom always said I had a hyperactive imagination, that I talked about friends that weren't there. Imaginary friends that would visit in the night. Strange, sure, but was this any different? I just needed to focus. Keep my thoughts away from Khalil. Keep my thoughts to myself. Then shove the *what if* away. The way Layla looked at me, drenched in nothing but pity, when I told her I thought I saw him in our room, I didn't need it. I wanted none of it. Layla couldn't begin to imagine what this felt like. And of course, I never wanted her to. As much as she was annoyed by her sisters, I knew how much she loved them. But if I could do without her pitying looks, then I would. And yet. The thought kept nagging at me.

What if.

What if.

What if.

"What if we went somewhere else first?"

"Like where?" They both turned around from a few steps ahead.

"This is going to sound crazy, but last night, right before I drove us into that ditch, I thought I saw someone in the middle of the road."

"Did you . . . hit some—" Ellis looked afraid to finish the sentence.

"No, God no. There might not have even been anyone there. I could be wrong. It all happened so fast and there was so much rain, but it looked like there was someone, or the shape of someone, in the middle of the road, and then nothing. I just. I really want to go back to where it happened and look around."

"For what though?" Layla asked. She looked confused, like she couldn't understand why I'd be so eager to go back. I wasn't entirely sure either. What would there be to even find? I just knew that the voice in my head wouldn't quiet until I answered.

I shrugged. "I just want to know if I saw what I saw."

They both looked at me, unsure of what to do, until Ellis finally spoke.

"Izzy can probably take us? We work together at the motel. You met her yesterday, Mira."

"That would be great," I said.

He nodded and walked a few yards away to make the call.

Layla turned to me, concern etched on her face. "You okay?"

I wasn't sure how to answer that, how honest to be. "I'm sure it's nothing. Just couldn't hurt to check, you know?"

She nodded and sat down on the curb, cradling her camera in her lap. Eventually, Ellis and I joined her as we waited for Izzy. A few minutes later, an old two-door yellow Ford Focus that had as much charm as it did rust pulled up in front of us.

Ellis stood up and walked over to the driver's side. The window was down, and they did a quick but intricate handshake before he walked around to the passenger side. We followed him.

"Ladies first," he said as he pulled the passenger seat forward to make room for us. We squeezed into the back seat, and Ellis pushed back his, locking it in place.

"I'm Izzy," she said as she started driving out of town. "Ellis's chauffeur and favorite person."

"I already said thank you," Ellis said, rolling his eyes. His tone was serious, but I could see he was smiling in the rearview mirror.

"Mm-hmm," she said, and turned her attention back to us. "So, where are we going?"

"Take a left here. It's the main road right outside of town, off I-65. I can let you know when to stop." At least I hoped I could. It was one long stretch of pavement, hard to nail down exactly where we crashed, but I could guess. Izzy made the turn and continued driving straight. We sat in the silence, watching the town disappear.

"I'm Layla and this is Mira, by the way," Layla said, trying to fill the silence. She was never good with the quiet.

"I figured as much when Ellis told me who was coming. You both look like your names. Ellis just didn't mention how pretty you both were."

I could see his face go red, but he didn't say anything, just toyed with the window switch as he watched the glass go up and down.

"Thanks," she mumbled.

"Are you guys together?" Izzy asked, and now it was Layla's turn to go bright red.

"What? No. Best friends. We're just best friends. Practically sisters!" She practically scooted to the opposite side of the car as she said it.

"How long have you been working at the motel?" I asked, changing the subject for Layla's sake.

"Six years now, I think. Right, Ellis? God, you were just a little kid then," she said, ruffling his hair. He swatted her hand away and laughed. "They grow up so fast. Started after I graduated high school, and now I'm in grad school working on my thesis over at Indiana University, in Bloomington. Maybe I'm the one that's grown." She let out one quick laugh before the smile fell.

After a while, she slowed down so I could figure out where we were last night. But everything looked the same. Just fields with woods in the distance on both sides. There was nothing distinguishable about any of it. Then a flash of light in the grass, a piece of glass glinting against the sun.

"There!" I said. She slammed the brakes and the car skidded to a halt in the middle of the road. She and Ellis got out, and Layla and I followed suit. This had to be it. I walked closer to the place where the glass glimmered against the light. I couldn't be sure the shattered shards were from my headlights, but the fresh tire tracks against the mud leading to them were proof enough.

"This is it," I told them.

"What should we do?" Layla asked.

"Just look around, I guess?" I don't think I could have given more unhelpful instructions, but I had no idea what I was looking for either. I knew I was being vague with everyone, but they didn't need to know how sure I was about what I'd seen. There was someone there and then there wasn't. I wouldn't have crashed the car for no reason. But I was getting enough *Is she crazy?* looks from everyone. I didn't need to back up the claims for them. We all spread out, aimlessly wandering the field in both directions. Ellis stayed close, and Layla and Izzy took the field across the road. I could hear Layla's camera clicking away every few

steps they took. Last night's rain had ended, but everything was still damp. I searched for any sign of someone, but there was nothing to be found. If there had been footprints, the rain had washed them away by now. If someone had been here, they hadn't dropped anything. They just disappeared into the mist.

I had wasted everyone's time, and even if I knew what I'd seen, I sure couldn't prove it.

"I don't see anything," Ellis said from a few feet away.

"Same," I said, walking over to him. Across the road, I could see Izzy and Layla engrossed in a conversation. Izzy laughed at what Layla was saying, and she quickly looked away, busying herself with the buttons on her camera. She took a step back and hid behind it, capturing Izzy with her head thrown back, a face full of joy. Her twists danced against her back and landed on her shoulder as she laughed. A hot-pink silk wraparound dress flowed over her like water. I would bet anything Layla captured her perfectly. Not just Izzy but the essence of Izzy.

"Should we grab them and get back?"

He nodded, and we crossed the road. They hadn't found anything either, which wasn't surprising. I couldn't help the disappointment that came trickling in though. Maybe I just needed to let it go. Whatever answers lived in the night before, they were gone now. Izzy drove us back into town

and dropped us off in front of the diner before she went to the library.

A bell above rang when Ellis opened the door for us. Inside, the diner had a wall lined with old red leather booths, some cracked at the seams. Small two-person tables were spread out in the middle of the room, and a counter rested on the other side. A glass case of pastries shone in the overhead light. The smell of almond croissants hit me as soon as I walked in. I slid into the booth across from Layla, and Ellis sat down next to me. The wallpaper held detailed illustrations of hundreds of birds, their names in cursive scrawled beneath each one. Some in midflight, others resting alone on branches or in pairs. I wanted to study each one of them, to learn every name on these walls.

Around us, people stared. At first, I thought they were looking at Layla and me. A small town, two girls they hadn't seen before. But that wasn't it. Their eyes quickly passed over us and settled on Ellis. He avoided them and kept his eyes trained on the menu. My mind went to what the mechanic had said. About the things that go bump in the night at the motel, the silent implication that people had died there in strange ways. Was he a social pariah because his family owned it?

"What am I doing? I know exactly what I'm getting." He smiled to himself and handed me the menu. "May I suggest the cheeseburger? It is not only edible but adequate."

"I've never said no to a cheeseburger. Layla, how about you?" She studied her menu, unsure of what to order. I had stopped eating halal years ago, but Layla was still on the fence, occasionally being a stickler for the no-pork and no-non-halal-meat rule and occasionally saying screw it and ordering anything she liked. Clearly, this place wouldn't have halal options, but after a few seconds, she closed the menu.

"Three cheeseburgers." She looked up then and noticed the stares, all the eyes trained on Ellis.

"Okay, is it just me, or is everyone staring at you?" she asked him. I wished I had told her what the mechanic said—maybe then she would have connected the dots and restrained herself from asking the question—but I hadn't. I'd kept it to myself because I didn't want to add fuel to the fire. I didn't need her to think that I believed the mechanic, like what he said was proof that what I saw was real, like I was convinced I was seeing my dead brother's ghost or something. I didn't need to be the sad, grieving girl who was seeing things. I mean, I was those things. But I didn't need her to wallow in it with me. To look at me with those *Poor you* eyes, like I was crazy. Maybe I was crazy. But either way, I didn't need to throw that on Layla. Besides, it was town legend. Nothing worth bringing up. I nudged her with my foot underneath the table and tried to signal to her with my eyes not to ask, but our best friend language was getting lost in translation. She looked at me, confused.

"It's a long story. Wouldn't want to bore either of you with it. Let's just say the people of this town are incapable of minding their own business."

Just then, the waiter came up to the table to take our order. He had a buzz cut, a stained apron tied at the waist, and a face that screamed *I need my shift to end*. Ellis placed our order, adding in a large curly fries for the table, and the boy left, only to come back a few seconds later and set down three glasses of water.

"We've got no place to be. Go on," Layla said, pushing a little further. Sometimes, I wished she knew when to let something rest. Ellis picked at his thumb, pulling at a hangnail. We waited.

"Okay. Sure. It's complicated. Well, just that people like to . . . talk, you know? They, it's . . ." He paused, took a deep breath, and laid his hands flat on the table.

"If you ask anyone here, they'll tell you that last winter, my mom killed my dad."

TEN

There is no one here. And yet, the Pull persists. Faint with Mira farther away, but it is undeniable, a thin thread that loops and winds and trails behind. Their luggage lies scattered between the two beds, clothes sprouting from both. Makeup litters the bathroom sink.

Beneath the noise of their presence, the marks they've made in this room, there is a pulse, a tone, a tremor in the air. Something is building, simmering just out of reach.

ELEVEN

Layla

Mira and I looked at each other, our eyes wide and full of questions.

"What do you mean, your mom killed your dad? The one we met yesterday? Elena?" I said.

"I didn't say she did it. She found him. Everyone is just convinced that she killed him too. Obviously, she'd be in prison or something if that was the case, but people don't care much for logic."

"Oh," I said. We sat with that for a minute until I pushed a little further. "What happened?"

"Where?" Mira asked at the same time. Her voice was quiet, hesitant.

"What?" Ellis said, turning to her.

"Where did she find him?"

His eyes focused on her. He looked surprised, but understanding washed over his face.

"Room 9."

"Excuse me," I said, jumping in, "Room 9 as in the room we're staying at? That Room 9? Buddy, no."

They both looked at me, unsure of what to say.

"What happened?" Mira asked this time.

He took a deep breath and said, "My dad had never been a happy man. It always seemed like you had turned the volume down around him, like when you looked at him, the world felt a little grayer or something. Nothing happened to set it off, I don't think. He just went into Room 9 one night and didn't come out. My mom eventually went to look for him and found him lying on the shower floor, an empty bottle of his sleeping pills next to him."

"My God, that's awful," I said. Mira looked sick next to him, like all the color had drained from her face.

"Just wait, I haven't even gotten to the really awful part yet." He laughed, but there was a bitter edge to it. "My mom left Room 9, locked the door behind her, and pretended everything was fine for three whole days."

Mira and I looked at each other, eyes wide. We let him continue.

"She told me he left on a trip or something? That he'd be back. She kept saying that. *He'll be back. He'll be back.* I remember thinking it was odd. My dad never went on trips. But I ignored it and holed up in my room like I always do.

A guest in the room next door eventually came in to complain about a smell, and I think that's what set my mom off. She started sobbing at the front desk and eventually called 911 and told them everything."

"Wow," I said.

"Yeah. And since this town loves to gossip, it didn't take long for everyone to find out she left him like that for three days."

We sat in the silence for a moment, no one knowing what to say next. The waiter came out with our burgers and set them down on the table, then made a second trip for the fries.

"Well, it was nice having two people who didn't know that about me while it lasted. Feel free to look at me with pity and or suspicion all you want now."

"Of course not," I said, but my face betrayed me. Mira, on the other hand, had a much better poker face and was convincingly neutral in her response.

"Screw 'em," she said. "If they've made up their mind about you or your family, it's not your job to change it."

He smiled at her, relief evident in his eyes. They kept looking at each other. Long enough that I felt like I was intruding just by being at the same table as them. Eventually he looked away and took a bite of his burger. I tried to eat mine, but I couldn't taste it. I didn't want to be upset. There was no use in being mad or sad or jealous or whatever this was. Mira was never mine to begin with. But no matter how many times I tried to swallow my feelings down with a bite of my cheeseburger, they came back up, adamant on rising to the surface.

The conversation shifted and Mira and Ellis talked about bands and books and movies. If it were any other situation, I would have jumped in with too many opinions, and maybe, just maybe, I would have even had a good time. But instead, I ate my burger silently, picked at a few curly fries, and let them learn new things about each other. I hated that I couldn't let her just be happy even if it wasn't because of me. It felt like a gut punch every time she laughed at a joke of his. Even if it was funny. Those only hurt more.

"Ready?" Mira asked me. I nodded and picked up my camera bag. We all paid for our food and headed out, with me trailing behind. I almost ripped his arm out of his socket when he placed his hand ever so gently on the small of her back. He was leading her out of the diner as if she weren't capable of finding the exit on her own. But I knew that if Mira didn't like it, she would have shrugged it off, made some effort to move away. And she didn't. She let his hand rest there until he no longer had a reason to touch her.

It was getting late at this point. The sun was low, and there was a chill in the air, a brisk breeze as we walked down the sidewalk. I took a few shots of the town as they walked

ahead of me. Mira turned around and looked at the camera, giving me a chance to get a shot she probably knew I wanted. I snapped it. I had a 35mm prime lens on, the only one I'd brought on the trip, and when I zoomed in on the screen, I could see how the light had hit her hazel eyes just right. Though gray in the black-and-white settings, they still shone in the sun.

Even the weird warping around her was starting to look a little cool, like maybe I could make it work to my advantage. Purposeful, even. Maybe if I updated my online portfolio, the School of the Art Institute of Chicago would find the photos interesting, stylistic and special. I couldn't rely on luck to get off their waitlist. I needed to show that I deserved that spot.

Mira lagged behind Ellis for a second, leaving him a few steps ahead of us, and weaved her arm around mine. With one touch, I forgot every shitty thought I had about Ellis.

"You okay?" she said. Her brow furrowed a bit.

"Yeah, just tired."

"I get it. Feels like it's been a long day and it's what?" she said, checking her phone. "Five? Damn, we're old." She chuckled.

"Maybe we can call it a night early and watch a movie in bed?" I asked, ready to bury the hatchet. I didn't like what Ellis was doing to me.

"Literally cannot think of anything more perfect," she said. We smiled at each other, let it linger for a second more than necessary. I wanted to apologize for being a jerk. My mouth began shaping the words, but then Ellis turned back and asked a question I didn't bother listening to, and as quickly as it had come, the moment was gone.

Finally, we said our goodbyes to Ellis at the office and made our way to our room. As soon as we stepped in, I couldn't help but picture what Ellis had told us, how his father's dead body sat in the shower for three days before anyone came for it.

"How did you know to ask where?" I said as I set my camera down. "Most people ask how or why. But you asked where. Like you already knew what he was going to say." She sat down on the bed and looked at me.

"The mechanic," she finally said.

"From town? What about him?"

"When I went in to ask about the car, he implied that people had died in the motel before, strange incidents with past guests, things he couldn't explain. I wondered if Ellis's dad was one of them."

"One of them? How many people died here? You didn't think to share that with me?"

"It didn't seem important, and I'm sure it's mostly town gossip anyway. Look at this place. This motel has been around for decades. Things are bound to happen. Plus, you heard Ellis. People just like to talk. It's fine."

I wanted to believe her, but she wouldn't meet my eyes. She seemed to look everywhere but at me. "What do you mean it didn't seem important? Someone died in this room. Lots of someones. In this motel." I wrapped my arms around myself, my eyes darting to each corner of the room. "Seems like information you should share if this motel is basically haunted. I'd rather not have ghosts or djinns or whatever watching me sleep."

"Don't even. You hate when our moms say shit like that. *It's a djinn. It's the evil eye.* It's bullshit. All it comes down to is I told you I saw my brother and you said that I clearly hit my head too hard. I didn't need you to look at me like I was crazy if I said this place was haunted too." Mira took a deep breath, closed her eyes for a second, and tried to deescalate the situation. I expected her to stay firm, to argue back, but she was good at being the bigger person when I couldn't be. "Ellis said it was fine. He's been here forever. I say we trust him over some gossip from the town mechanic."

I knew she was giving me an out. I could let it go. I should let it go. But after this morning, I couldn't help but push a little further, like a part of me wanted to make a mess of this, wanted to see it crumble.

"Just because Ellis says it's fine doesn't mean I don't need to know," I said.

"What is going on right now?" she said quietly. "What does any of it matter? You don't believe in this haunted shit. You never have. And Ellis is a nice guy; you've been rude to him since we met him. I don't get what your problem is."

"That's not the point. My problem is you're getting way too friendly with this guy we barely know and keeping things from me."

"Ellis has been nothing but kind to both of us since we met him. I'm sorry I didn't tell you what the mechanic said. Be mad about that if you need to be, but you have to let the Ellis stuff go. You are not the only person I'm allowed to have in my life."

I bristled at that, struck by her words. That's when I should have pulled back, stopped pushing.

"It's not about that."

She paused, studying me. Finally, she said, "Then what is it about? Is there something you want to say to me?"

And in that moment, I could feel it in the air. The offer. To admit that what this was really about was jealousy. Pathetic, predictable jealousy. My cheeks flamed at the thought that she might have seen through me all along. That she had known and chosen to ignore every desperate sign that seeped out of me without my permission. I wondered how different things would be if I came out and said it. If I came out. But I didn't want to mess this up, and I couldn't be gay, not if I wanted to speak to my family ever again, and I wanted I wanted I wanted for so many things, Mira most of all, but I couldn't have any of them, so I took a step back and spat out, "Ever since last summer, you've thrown yourself at every guy and girl who's looked at you for more than two seconds. I shouldn't be surprised that Ellis is no different."

I regretted it the moment I said it. But the echo of my words hung in the air, and neither of us could ignore what had spilled from my mouth. She didn't say anything. She just turned around and walked out, leaving the door wide open.

TWELVE

Mira

A few doors down, I paused and took a deep breath, trying to inhale as much of the evening air as I could. I was tired of fighting with Layla, of the awkwardness that had settled between us since this morning. It felt heavy, having to carry it. How had this all escalated so quickly? I didn't understand. One second we were talking about ghosts, and the next, I don't even know what. The rest aside, I guess she'd accused me of exactly what I was doing. I thought about every person I'd gone out with in the last year, a poor attempt to lose myself in something aside from my own grief. I didn't want her to be right, but we both knew exactly when this started.

When Khalil died, we couldn't afford to fly his body back to America, so we settled for a small ceremony with our extended family. None of his friends or our family friends. No one who truly knew him but us three. We were all staying in my grandmother's house for the summer, and

I remember my mom coming into my room the morning of the funeral and quietly brushing my hair back into a bun because I didn't have it in me to wash it. Her face was stoic in the mirror, stripped of any emotion. I knew what she'd be like if she let that wall go. If her grip slipped from whatever edge she was barely hanging on to. I'd never forget the image of her screaming in the sand, the veins in her neck pulsing as she let out a gut-wrenching cry that made even the seagulls quiet.

I closed my eyes, but it was printed on the back of my lids, as inescapable as our grief. She didn't say anything as she tied my hair back. Just patted me on the shoulder when she was done and walked away. The car ride to the mosque was just as quiet. A procession of cars slowly made its way down the road. My dad fiddled with the radio for a few minutes until he gave up and turned it off. His red-rimmed eyes looked back at me from the rearview mirror, and I glanced away. Most of what came next was a blur. People praying. A line of my extended family's neighbors and friends giving their condolences for a boy they never knew.

I watched as an aunt gripped my hands and said something about God's plan.

I watched as my mother thanked her sister for me when I just stood there, motionless, until she moved on.

I watched as the men carried my brother's casket outside to the neighboring cemetery.

All I did was watch. It didn't feel like I was really there anymore. I was a ghost of myself. Maybe now I could see him, Khalil, watching over his own funeral, rolling his eyes at the hysterical neighbors who had met him once five years ago. But he wasn't here, and I was a copy of a copy of myself while I watched people I barely knew wail as Khalil's body was lowered into the ground. I couldn't help but notice his casket was smaller than the ones I had seen in movies, that my brother's body would cease to grow and overtake me in height and weight like we always knew he would. As I get older, I'll never have him as a point of reference. The car ride back was just as quiet. My dad parked, and I let them walk ahead of me to go inside, where their friends and our family would be waiting.

Chairs were set up outside the house, men seated there staring at the ground, somber guards to the mourning that was happening beyond those doors. But I couldn't get past them. I couldn't walk inside and face the pitying looks and the sobbing strangers, as if their shallow grief was performance for our viewing pleasure. I just couldn't. One of the men looked up at me, his brow furrowed, waiting for me to step inside. I didn't know him. A neighbor or something maybe. He nodded at me as if he understood, and that was all I needed. I ran. All the way back to the main street that held the bustling shops and storefronts. I didn't have a plan aside from not being in that house. I stepped into a coffee shop that was playing a soccer game and took a seat at a table in the back.

Women didn't come to coffee houses here, not alone and not during soccer matches. But I didn't have it in me to care.

"What team are you rooting for?" a boy a table over said in Arabic. He looked my age, a little older maybe, and he was sitting alone with a near-empty glass of tea in front of him.

"Chelsea," I said, picking the team that was down by one goal.

His hand went to his chest with a soft thud as he closed his eyes. "A girl after my heart," he said.

I laughed, surprising myself with the sound. We watched in silence for a few minutes.

"It's not looking good for our team," he said, motioning toward the TV as Chelsea tried and failed to score a goal.

"It's not too late to change sides."

He gasped, appalled by my suggestion. "Never. I'm offended you would even suggest that. I thought I knew you better."

"Goes to show. You never really know anyone."

"Do you really think that?"

I paused, considering. "I don't know."

"Well, I hope not. It seems like an empty way to live life." He swallowed the rest of his tea and set a few coins down on the table. The match wasn't over yet, but he stood up and tucked his chair back in.

"It was nice meeting you, Chelsea."

I smiled up at him and that was that. He walked away and eventually rounded the corner. I never saw him again. But the second he was out of view, I realized that however briefly, I had forgotten about my own grief for the first time in two days. At a time where I was swallowed up by it, I didn't even know it was possible to step away for a few seconds. That a flirty conversation with a boy I didn't know was enough to keep my mind away from the only thing it kept wanting to return to. It hadn't gone far. Nothing had happened, not really, anyway, and yet it felt like an epiphany. One I spent the next year exploiting.

And Layla saw everything. She saw the way I had changed since coming back, the ways I avoided any difficult conversations or jumped from one person to the next. All to avoid thinking about the one person who was the cause of all this. She watched as I withdrew into myself in every way that mattered. I'd used people to run from grief, and the moment it caught up with me, I left for the next crush who could keep my attention. In the process, I'd left her all alone.

It had been a little while now, and I didn't want to go back into the room. To sit in heavy silence until we fell asleep. I walked to the edge of the motel and rounded the corner where the pool was.

"Back already?" Ellis said. He was splayed out on a pool chair, one earbud in his left ear, the other resting on his chest. I shook my head at him. I was in no mood for jokes or company, but this motel was small, and his family owned it. Didn't make much sense to tell him to leave me alone. I lay down in the pool chair next to him and stared up at the setting sky.

I would be crazy to think that our fight was just about my dating history or Ellis or ghosts. I wondered if she was jealous, if it was the kind of jealousy that stemmed from something more than friendship. But it was no use. I didn't know what I expected from Layla. Layla wouldn't even disappoint her parents by telling them she was serious about majoring in photography, let alone going out of state for it. Which is how I knew that even if she felt anything toward me, she'd never do anything about it. Not if it meant potentially losing her family.

"Are you okay?" he asked after a few moments. I rubbed my eyes with the heels of my hands and looked up at the sky. The sun still hadn't set yet, but the sky was stained in reds and purples. Ellis laid his hand on my shoulder. I looked at him for a second, saw the concern etched on his face. I noted the way I wanted to lean into his hand, to let myself forget.

"Do you miss your dad?" I asked him.

He paused before answering. I could see the pain flicker in his eyes as he pulled his hand away.

"We weren't close, but I could feel how much of him had been there only after he was gone. I had been used to his quiet presence my whole life. I didn't know a life without him. And then suddenly I did. I don't think I realized how different it would be until it was."

"I don't want to say I'm sorry for your loss, because it's empty and I've always hated that. But I also don't know what else to say." I shrugged.

"Maybe that's why it's the only thing people think to say. It would be real quiet without it."

"Maybe that's fine too," I said. "To sit in silence with someone and let their grief wash over the both of you."

He smiled at me, leaned back in his chair, and closed his eyes. I followed suit, and we both sat there and let grief have its moment. Five minutes, ten, I didn't know. It was almost soothing, letting the weight of it all take its place, front and center. Eventually, I broke the silence.

"My little brother died last year." I could hear him twist around to look at me, but I kept my eyes closed, kept my breathing steady. Everyone in my life already knew this. And for a little while, I was adamant on making him the only person who didn't. I was tired of the pitying looks from kids at school, from neighbors, even from Layla. Every look was a reminder of what I lost, and most days, it seemed to be all anyone ever saw. The hushed whispers when I walked into the class. The forced smiles and furrowed brows from family friends. I was sick of all of it. But as soon as he told us about his dad, I knew he might understand in a way no one else had been able to. Not even Layla. I kept going. "We were overseas, visiting family in Tunisia, when it happened. I only have the one brother. Had. Anyway, my parents and us, we spent the day at the beach, and my brother wasn't much of a swimmer. He had taken lessons as a kid, sure, but it never stuck, you know?" I opened my eyes to look at him and he nodded at me, waiting for me to go on.

"I don't mind the water, but I stick to pools, the occasional lake back in Michigan, but the sea is different. The sea is moody and temperamental and can swallow you up whole if it wants to. We're nothing to the sea." I could feel my breathing getting shallower. I took a deep breath, forced it into every inch of my lungs, and skipped to the end. "It all happened so fast. By the time someone noticed what was happening, he had stopped breathing. He was only fourteen." I could feel Ellis wanting to say something, but instead, he resisted and sat in the silence with me, letting it fill the space between us.

Suddenly, I remembered the morning of his death, a morning I was sure I had forgotten. I had come out of the water to find Khalil eating a slice of watermelon on the sand. The beach umbrella was tipped back, no longer blocking the sun like it had been an hour ago, but I didn't mind. I sat down next to my mom, feeling the hot sand against my bare legs. I dug my wet hands in, letting it sift through my fingers. To her left, my dad had one hand blocking the sun from his eyes, and near the other was a book in Arabic. Something about politics and God that he had planned to read but that now lay abandoned, half-buried in the sand.

"Mira, you need more sunscreen. Look at you. Your shoulders are burned," my mother said in Arabic. She grabbed the bottle and smeared the sunscreen on my shoulders, adding until she was satisfied. She put the bottle away and started digging around in the cooler we'd brought.

"Hungry? I have watermelon, sandwiches, ice cream, some brik from last night." She moved around a few more things. "Aha, those cookies you like! I also made lemonade, but I think you should eat something first." She looked at me, waiting. I could see my brother shake his head and smile at me from behind her. I grabbed a slice of water-melon and went to sit next to him before she could protest that it wasn't enough to eat.

"What are you reading?" I asked, switching to English. It always felt odd talking to him in Arabic. I don't know why. Sure, neither of us could read or write it, but we both understood it, even if I spoke it a little better. I always spoke Arabic with my parents, but he somehow got away with replying to their Arabic in English every time. They stopped fighting it years ago, and I guess neither of us wanted to make the effort when it felt more natural to switch languages when we were together. He had his left arm with the rind outstretched away from the book, making sure that the watermelon juices weren't dripping on the pages. He flipped to the cover to show me the title.

"*The Raven Boys*, about a group of friends trying to find a sleeping king. Really good so far." He set it down to focus on the watermelon. "How's the water?" he asked around a mouthful.

"Warm. Inviting. You'd know if you came in," I said, bumping him with my shoulder.

"Why bother when you can tell me all about it?"

"Oh, come on, it's not so bad. We won't even go that far in."

"Last weekend you got stung by a jellyfish literally three

feet from shore. I don't think distance saves you from any-thing, Mira." He placed the watermelon rind on the sand and wiped his hands on his dry dark navy shorts.

"That was a different beach! And totally on me. I saw it and just didn't think it would sting me?" I rubbed the inside of my calf, the memory of the burn still fresh in my mind. "Anyway, I doubt this beach has jellyfish too."

"Listen to your sister," my dad said without moving. "We only have one more week before we go back. You're going to regret not swimming all summer. Nothing better than Mediterranean waters."

My brother sighed and threw himself back on the sand.

"I'll meet you in the water. Let me just finish my chapter."

"Okay, I'm trusting you. I'll see you in there."

I could hear my mom yelling at him about sunscreen as I ran back to the water. My skin was warm from the sun, and the water felt refreshing against it. I remember plung-ing into the sea and staying under for as long as I could hold my breath.

"You know, I still see him sometimes, in the shape of someone's shoulders, the way a stranger walks across the street," I said to Ellis, finally breaking the silence. "I had the weirdest, most surreal moment this morning, when I thought I saw him sitting there, his back to me, then he just disappeared. Not like I blinked and he was gone, like he dissolved into smoke or something." I tried to laugh it off, but it was caught in my throat. I had spent this entire day trying to brush it off, to convince myself what I saw was not what I thought: that my imagination was dark and twisted and a clear sign that I was going crazy. Like truly, fully crazy. I was tired of lying to myself. Of repeatedly quieting the voice that said, *What if you trusted what you saw.*

For a second in the diner, I'd thought maybe this wasn't my doing. That I didn't have to worry about trusting my own mind. Maybe there was something bigger than me that I couldn't explain. But that thought was crazier than I probably was. I held my head in my hands, my fingers weaving into my curls. "I swear, Ellis, sometimes I can't tell the difference between grief and insanity."

"Where?" he whispered, and there it was, that echo. A question and an answer in one. I looked at him, about to respond, but he already knew. "It's always that room," he said.

"Specifically Room 9? Not the motel? The mechanic said the whole place was basically haunted."

He nodded, confirming. "Nothing has ever happened in the other rooms. Not that I can recall. It's why I didn't want to give you guys the reservation. I—I don't know. There's something I've never been able to understand about that room."

My heart raced at the idea of what he was implying. I tried to piece it together. Was something happening? Khalil sitting on the bed? The shape against the shower glass? This constant feeling of being watched? But knowing this, that maybe I wasn't insane after all, wasn't necessarily better. What was in that room?

"Can I show you something?" he said. He didn't wait for me to get up. I could sense his nervous excitement in his hurried steps and tense shoulders. I jogged to catch up to him as he led me into the office.

"Hey, Izzy, your shift just start?" Ellis said. She set her book down, the same one Ellis had been reading this morning, and smiled.

"Elly, hey! Yeah, just got here. Short shift tonight, at least. Hey, Mira," she added.

"We're going to go upstairs for a bit. Don't tell my mom, okay?" He whispered this last part, but I was standing right there. It was impossible not to hear.

"I got you," she said with a wink. "Nice to see you again, Mira."

"You too," I said, and followed Ellis upstairs. I wondered, for a passing moment, if this was his weird, elusive way of making a move. He opened the door for me, and I couldn't help but raise an eyebrow. His cheeks flushed, and he rushed to explain.

"No, no, nothing like that! I just— It's best that I show you, that's all." The blush crept into his neck as he stumbled over his words, trying to explain his pure intentions.

"I didn't say anything. Lead the way."

I followed him down a long hallway that led into a living room with a kitchen and table behind it. It was small. Quaint. The couch tattered at the edges, the appliances decades old. There was a purple stain at the edge of the rug the couch rested on. The wooden coffee table was chipped on the corners, and it had a stack of books in the center. No fancy coffee table books, from what I could see. Just broken spines and dog-eared pages on all of them. Framed pictures of Ellis were neatly placed on the windowsill. His mom appeared in a few, holding a baby Ellis, both of them at a park, but I couldn't see any of his dad, almost like he had been erased. Still, aside from that detail, the place looked lived in. Loved.

"I didn't realize you lived here," I said once we were in his room.

"Yeah. The second floor is an apartment, so it only made sense. I've lived here my whole life."

I nodded, checking out his room. His blue bedcovers were rumpled. The bookshelves were packed full, not a single space wasted. As if that wasn't enough, he had a pile next to his bed and another near his wooden desk. Most of the piled books had library stickers on the spine. The surface of his desk was surprisingly clean. A laptop, a lamp, and an empty cup rested in the center. A yellow notebook and a pen rested on the edge, near his bed. He saw me taking it all in and straightened up his sheets. He quickly jumped to right a tower of books that leaned too far to the left.

"Sorry, it's sort of a mess."

"It's fine. Pristine compared to my room back home."

"Ha, okay, that makes me feel a little better." He chuckled nervously. His hand closed tightly around one of the doorknobs to his closet doors.

"Okay. So, this might seem a little weird. Just let me explain first."

"Enough buildup, Ellis. Let's see it."

He took a deep breath and twisted the doorknob, pulling it all the way open so that I could see what was on the other side.

THIRTEEN

Mira storms into the room. She is out of breath, vibrating with energy. The feelings that were plucked out of her like an amenable violin less than an hour ago have diminished. It was easy then. Emotions high, simmering just below the surface. There was barely any work to be done. One tug here, another pinch there. It was enough.

But now, the Pull hesitates, confused. Something has changed, and it doesn't quite understand what. It slivers through Mira, stretching stems in new directions, trying to find cracks in her new surface. But Mira pushes back, only a little. She feels it though, this presence, everything a little heavier, time a little slower, as soon as she enters.

She continues.

"Layla, listen. I have to tell you something," she says.

The girl has been pacing since Mira left the room. Her distress is palpable, delectable, but it is a drop, insufficient. It quenches nothing. She whips around at the sound of Mira's voice and walks toward her.

"No, no. You listen. I'm sorry. I shouldn't have said that. It wasn't even true. I was just angry and—"

"It was a little true," Mira says, wincing at her own words. She goes on. "But it's fine. I'm not mad. Apology accepted. I need you to listen to me, okay?" She sits at the edge of the bed, waiting for an answer. She tries her best to stay focused, to do what she came to do, but she finds it difficult. Like wading through quicksand. Fighting it isn't always the best option.

"Okay? What's going on? You're acting really weird."

"Layla, I'm begging you. I need you to trust me. To listen. Please."

The other girl looks at her with wide eyes and nods. "I'm listening."

She sits up straighter.

Mira pauses for a second, trying to put words to feelings, to focus on the right words, the right feelings, but she senses the overwhelming nature of it all, looming all around her.

"Don't you feel it?" she asks.

"Feel what?"

"This place," Mira says, looking around. "There's something bad here. Something awful and dark. I thought I was imagining things, that I was grieving or going crazy, but what if I'm not?"

"Okay, go on."

"I was just with Ellis. Don't make that face."

"Sorry."

"I was just with Ellis, and he showed me something. Don't raise an eyebrow at me. I'm serious. I need you to come. He'll explain everything. Let's go."

Mira grabs the girl's hand and they run out, closing the door behind them, but this Pull has never been put off by doors, by barriers; this Pull stretches and curves. Only so far, yes, but it is not as easily escapable as Mira hopes.

FOURTEEN

Layla

"Well, shit."

"Yeah," they both said.

I leaned in closer, studying. Ellis had documented a history of Room 9 on the inside of his closet door. He had drawn a vertical timeline in permanent marker, starting from 1976 at the bottom and traveling up to the last death. Every few years, the timeline would branch off with a new name, indicated by a sticky note and a photo or newspaper article he had tracked down. A total of eight deaths in half as many decades. Some faceless, some not.

"I only started doing this a few months ago, after my dad died. I just needed to understand. I'm not even sure what. But there's something there. I'm just not seeing it."

I read through the notes he had listed around each name. Where in the room they were found, how they died, the length of their stay. But nothing overlapped.

"Do you mind?" I asked, holding up my phone to take a picture.

"Go for it," he said. Something about his detailed work, the lives taped to the door, the secrecy of it being hidden away and how desperate he was for us to see it all, to believe him—I needed to capture some small emblem of it.

"I can't believe you gave us a room a bunch of people died in," I said. Mira sat cross-legged on his gray rug, pulling at the short threads near her feet. He was perched on the edge of his bed, looking at us both. He seemed unsure of how to defend himself.

"I know, I know. I'm sorry. I didn't want to, I swear. You guys seemed nice. Not that I wouldn't have minded if you guys didn't seem nice," he said, quickly backtracking. "I just mean I didn't have much of a choice. My mom. She's worried about vacancy, needs the rooms to be booked to make ends meet. And she doesn't believe me about Room 9. Thinks it's all a coincidence." He held his head in the palms of his hands, his fingers wound into the strands of his dark hair. He was quiet for a moment. "I don't know what to do." He sighed and looked up at his door, his eyes scanning the faces taped there. "I just know if I figured out what's connecting all of them, maybe I could understand why he did it. Maybe I could figure out something that makes this all make sense."

Mira and I looked at each other. I knew we were deciding, right then and there, if we were diving deeper into whatever this was or packing our things and spending the

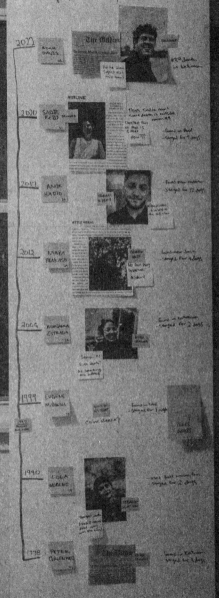

NOAH
DAVIS

42

The Wildw

Beloved Motel Owner Di

Did he
Signed Pu
Miss Ben?

RIBUNE

SADIE
REID   DROWNED

31

SADIE REID
DROWNED
DEAD AT 31

How???

AMIR
HADID   34

STARVED
TO DEATH

next two nights at some bed-and-breakfast in town. If we were desperate, the back seat of her broken-down car was also an option.

She nodded, almost imperceptibly, and I knew we were seeing this through. At least as much as we could before we had to leave on Friday.

"Okay," I said. "Tell us what we need to know."

He looked at us, his eyes jumping from me to Mira and back again. "You guys believe me? You think there's something in that room too? Because if I have to hear that this is an unhealthy way to grieve my father's death one more time, I'm going to scream."

"Your mom?" Mira asked.

He nodded.

"Well, we're not your mom. Some weird shit is happening, and I want to figure it out too. So, let's hear it. What have you learned in making your serial-killer wall?" she said. He narrowed his eyes at her but chose to ignore the comment.

He stood up, and I took his spot on the bed.

"My family bought this place in the late nineties. At the time, there had only been two deaths. But since this motel opened in 1976, eight people have died in Room 9." He pointed to the names up the door as he said them. "Peter, Lola, Eugene, Marianna, Maya, Amir, Sadie, and Noah."

He stumbled over the last one, as if the N got caught on his tongue, hitting the back of his teeth, like he had to push it out.

"They happen further apart at first. Twelve years between the first two. And then nine, and seven, and less and less as time goes by until the next death. Time isn't a pattern, unless you count that the deaths are happening closer and closer to one another every time. Length of stay also isn't a factor. I checked our records. Some stayed one night, others over a week."

"What about the deaths themselves? How did the people die?" I asked.

He shrugs. "No real pattern there either. Peter slipped in the shower and hit his head on the bathroom sink and bled out before anyone found him. Lola hanged herself from the fan. Eugene died in his sleep, but he was seventy-three. Marianna also slipped in the shower. Maybe we should be using less slippery tile. I'm not sure. Maya was found with her neck snapped, though no foul play was suspected, and Amir starved himself to death. Sadie, though, drowned in the pool. Does that death count, since it wasn't technically in the room? Good question. I've decided to count it. She spent an entire week in that room, and that pool is five feet at its deepest."

I couldn't help but notice that he stopped before the eighth death. No need to rehash his own father's details.

"Okay, so if there's no connection between their deaths and length of time in the room, what about the people? Any patterns there?" Mira asked.

"Ages range from Lola's nineteen to Eugene's seventy-three. Their races varied, as did their jobs, backgrounds, and, from what I could gather, the reasons they chose to stay here." He sat back down on the bed, and I shuffled over to make room for him. He threw himself back and stared at the ceiling. "There's nothing connecting anything. And they're all dead, so it's not like I can ask follow-up questions, you know? Hi, Eugene, are you a coincidence, or are there no coincidences in Room 9? Why did you kill yourself, Lola? How in the world did you drown in five feet of water, Sadie? The dead are dead ends."

I patted his leg awkwardly and got up to give him room. It was a twin bed, and he was a tall-enough guy.

"What I'm hearing is for the first time, you have actual guests staying in Room 9 who know things are happening in it. Guests who you can ask anything you want, right?" Mira asked.

He nodded.

"Then let's hear it. What are your burning questions?" Mira stretched out her legs, getting comfortable on the rug. She looked up at him and smiled.

"Really? Okay, cool. One second."

He leaned forward and grabbed the yellow notebook and pen from over Mira's head. The door creaked open as he turned to an empty page. Ellis's mom poked her head in, surprise clear on her face as she took in the scene. Her son taking notes. Mira spread out on the floor. Me standing next to the centerpiece of his room: Ellis's Eight Deaths of Room 9 Research. Her lips pursed when her eyes found the door.

"Ellis, can I speak with you? Right now."

She didn't wait for him before leaving. His face burned red, but he got up and followed her out. Mira and I looked at each other, both straining to hear the conversation on the other side of the wall.

"First of all, you can't have girls in your room without asking. You know the rules. You talk to me first and the door stays open. And second, what are you doing showing anyone that ridiculous door, let alone guests who are currently staying with us? How does that make sense to you? We can't afford vacancies right now. Do you want them to leave?"

"Yes. Something is happening in that room. They said so themselves. I didn't even bring it up. They *should* leave."

"Then their room rate can come out of your paycheck. Or better yet, I can let Izzy go, since I don't know how you expect me to keep paying her when you're constantly trying to turn people away. You can't keep doing this, Ellis. You just can't."

Neither said anything for a few seconds. We waited in the silence with them.

"This isn't good for you. Not after last time." She said this quietly, quieter than the rest. He didn't respond, or if he did, we couldn't hear it. She eventually continued.

"They can stay for a little while. But enough talk about the room. It's not haunted. It's just plain bad luck."

Ellis came back in after that. He nudged the door nearly closed, an unspoken compromise.

"Let's try to be quiet, okay?" he said into his notebook. "My mom's being annoying. Now, where were we?"

I looked at Mira, wondering if we should ask.

"What did your mom mean, 'not after last time'?" I said, deciding for us.

He looked at us both, his eyes wide, unsure. He sighed.

"After my dad died, I had to see a therapist. I wasn't handling it well, I guess. I don't know. I think my mom just didn't like the way I was grieving. Learning about this room helped me, dug me out of a hole of depression. But I got caught up, hyperfocused. I stayed in my room for weeks. I didn't sleep. I barely ate. I needed to learn everything I could about Room 9. She got concerned, made me get help. The therapist said I was using this to avoid dealing with my own grief, and who knows, he could be right. My mom thinks I'm better because of him—who I do like talking to, that's not it," he said, raising his hands to make his point. "But the only reason I'm not holed up in my room anymore is because I've hit a wall. There's nothing else I can learn about the room that isn't on that door or in this notebook."

I glanced at Mira, unsure of what to do with all that information.

She leaned forward and squeezed his hand.

"It's a good thing we're here," she said. "What do you want to know?"

He smiled at her and she smiled back. I could see him squeeze her hand before releasing it. My eyes were trained on their hands, on the quick clasp before letting go. What I needed to do was let *them* go. Mira had never shown any interest in me, not in the way I'd hoped. Not that I could have done anything about it. Maybe it was for the best that what I felt would never be reciprocated. Yet even sound logic couldn't stop me from feeling hurt when I saw her with anyone else. I would find a way to put this aside. To accept my situation and to focus on the one at hand. What good did it do to dwell on what could never be mine?

"I guess my first question is what's it like inside the room."

"What do you mean? Have you never been inside?" I asked him.

"No. Lately, when I walk past it, I can almost feel it. Or the way it makes me feel? Dark and anxious? As a kid, I always avoided going inside the rooms. Izzy has been working here for a few years, so she and my parents always cleaned them, and even when I started working the front desk, I always managed to keep my distance. It was more habit than anything else. I had heard the rumors growing up, scary stories that kids in town made up. A part of me didn't believe them. The rest of me found no reason to go in there and see. And then my dad died, and I couldn't bring myself to go inside that room for . . . well, obvious reasons."

We sat in that silence for a few seconds until I broke it. "It just feels like a motel room." I looked at Mira, waiting for her to answer.

"Overwhelming," Mira said quietly.

"Okay. How?" Ellis said, turning to her.

"Like it's hard to breathe in there? Like it's heavy and time is slower. Always in the present? Clearly time doesn't stop in there. I go to sleep and I wake up and it's the next day, but it feels . . . I don't know. Like there's only now and now and now, and it just keeps weighing you down, this idea of being watched in a place that won't let you go."

I looked at her, aware that there was nothing I could do to help her and hoping anyway.

"So, I guess my next question is, why don't you feel any of that, Layla?"

I shrugged. I didn't understand any of this. Sure, it felt weird being in that room knowing his dad died in it. Even weirder still knowing seven other people died too. But the room wasn't inherently odd or eerie. It was just a room.

I answered honestly. "I don't know."

He turned back to Mira. "You said you saw your brother there. What was he doing?"

She glanced at me quickly, but turned back to Ellis. "Drowning, I guess. Dying. The first time he was just sitting there, his back to me on the bed. The second time I could see him in the mirror, the shape of him against the shower glass. I couldn't see through it, but I could tell it was him. I don't know, I just knew. The way you know something in a dream. I didn't doubt it. It seemed like he or it or whatever was in pain." Mira hugged her knees to her chest. "You guys think I'm crazy, don't you?"

"We wouldn't be sitting here if we thought that," Ellis said. He reached out with a comforting hand and gently squeezed her knee. She smiled at him in response, and eventually, after way too long, if you ask me, he took his hand away.

I needed to be the comforting listener, but instead, Ellis was doing a much better job at it. I let my hesitation get the best of me, but who could blame me. I wanted so badly to believe. I just didn't know how.

"So, the only pattern we see is that people keep dying, and they're dying faster and faster," I said, trying to get us back on track.

"Death seems like the central theme here, right? Your research seems to say as much," Mira said. "I mean, sure, we don't know if it's my brother's ghost or if the room is some portal for people who haven't moved on, people we carry with us. Or maybe there's nothing there and it's just in my head, and I've brought you all into my insanity with me." She stopped and laughed for a second. "Talk about unhealthy ways to grieve, am I right, Ellis?"

He smiled but didn't say anything.

"Let's say something *is* happening in that room. We've got a first-person account. What now?" I said.

We all looked at one another, wondering what the next move was.

"What about an experiment?" he asked.

"You're going to have to be more specific," I said.

"You were alone when those things happened, Mira. But what if you were there waiting with Layla?" He turned to me. "If you stayed up, you could be there to confirm everything that Mira's seeing. We'd know if this is real or—"

"Or if it's all in my head and the only pattern in that room is coincidence," Mira said.

"And if it is real?" I asked.

"Then we'll figure that out in the morning. One stupid idea at a time, ladies."

Mira and I looked at each other. I could see her swallow, could read the fear in her eyes, plain as day. But she squared her shoulders and didn't look away. As scared as she was, I knew that when Mira decided on something, it was as good as done. There would be no convincing her otherwise. And even though I wanted to be logical about this, to remind them that they were taking this too far, that in a day, we would be on our way out of Wildwood, I also knew that I would never leave her to do this on her own. I nodded. No use fighting the immovable force that was Mira. We were pulling this all-nighter.

"What have we got to lose but our lives. We're in," Mira said.

"You know, you guys don't have to do this. You don't have to go back to that room if you don't want to."

"What are we going to do? Walk all the way to that bed-and-breakfast in the middle of the night?" I said, doing my best impression of a supportive best friend.

"You could stay here," he said more to himself than anyone else. "I mean, you guys could take the bed and I can sleep on the floor and we can forget this whole plan. You don't have to do this." He said that last part to Mira, and I hated it. Hated the way he looked at her, the way she seemed to like it. But how many chances had I blown with her? How many openings, imagined or not, had I shut down? I wasn't willing to do anything about my own feelings for her, so who was I to stand in the way of whatever this was? God, why did my brain have to keep focusing on them when it had so much more important things to obsess about? I watched as their eyes locked for a long second before she shook her head.

"No, your mom would come in and murder us. So, if you think about it, our lives are in danger either way. Might as well try to get to the bottom of this." She smiled, but it looked forced and distracted, barely reaching her eyes. It was starting to sink in what we were going back to. Most of me still thought this was one weird-ass coincidence. Just one clumsy or troubled or unfortunate guest after another. The room was a room and both Mira and Ellis were dealing with death in unhealthy but understandable ways. And then this tiny little voice inside my head whispered, *Trust Mira.* Even though she doubted herself, she believed there was something darker behind all of this. That needed to be enough. And so, until we could prove otherwise, until we could find some reasonable explanation for the unexplainable, I willed myself to believe, attempting to balance between logic and blind faith.

"Now that we have a plan, can I use your bathroom?" Mira asked.

"Sure, it's just back down the hall, the last door on the left."

She stood up and tiptoed out of the room, making sure to look both ways as if his mom were an oncoming car to watch for.

Ellis and I sat in the silence, looking everywhere but at each other. We had spent the day together, but it was Mira who made that happen. And sure, maybe if he didn't clearly like Mira, I wouldn't have found his presence so grating, but he did and so I did.

"Do you think Mira's okay? Like, really okay with going back, or . . ." He let the sentence drift. I tried to find anything but genuine concern in his face, but he seemed sincere. I sighed. It was exhausting hating this boy for existing. He'd done nothing but be nice to us, even if he was a little nicer with Mira. But who could blame him? And if she did like him too, who could blame either of them? He was cute, in this Timothée Chalamet sort of way. His dark hair was a nice contrast against his brown eyes, and even I could admit that he had a kind smile. She could do worse than Ellis—I knew that. I just hated admitting that my problem with him had nothing to do with him. I thought back to our fight from earlier, to Mira saying I wasn't the only person she was allowed to have in her life. And she was right. I couldn't come between her and the rest of the world. No matter how much I wanted to. No matter how much it hurt to see her happy with anyone else. Especially when all I ever did was wallow in this torment of my own making.

"Yeah. Plus, she won't be alone. We'll come right back here if anything weird happens," I said. I smiled, hoping it would ease the awkwardness, and he smiled back. It was almost like we were friends. If only it were that easy.

THURSDAY

FIFTEEN

Mira

We sat in a semicircle eating cold spaghetti that Ellis had snuck back for us.

"Sorry I didn't heat it up. It's almost one in the morning and if my mom heard the microwave, you guys would have had to go."

"It's fine. I prefer cold pasta," I said.

Layla moved the food around on her plate, as if annoyed that it was there. I nudged the parmesan toward her. Cheese always made her feel better. We went over the plan one more time. It was simple: Stay up. Wait. Watch. If both of us saw . . . it, then how could we deny it? We'd meet up the next morning for breakfast and go over what we learned. If anything. It wasn't much, but it was all we had for now, and it was the furthest Ellis had gotten with his research.

"I could stay with you guys, if you wanted. Can't hurt to have one more person in there, right?"

I looked at his sad eyes. I knew I couldn't let him do it.

He had never been inside, so why have him spend the night in the room his father killed himself in? It felt cruel to take him up on it.

"We got this. If anything dangerous happens, we'll call you."

He nodded. I could see his relief as his shoulders relaxed. We all exchanged numbers then, and when it felt like all we were doing was avoiding making our way back, we said our goodbyes.

It had been tempting, falling asleep there. Not having to think about some looming presence that attached itself to your back. Maybe I should have said yes to Ellis's offer to stay with him, but I knew Layla wouldn't have wanted to. Layla, who had made her feelings on Ellis perfectly clear and was only trying to play nice for my sake. She didn't want to sleep in his room, and she definitely didn't want him staying in ours. We would do this on our own.

And we had to do this. Nothing had felt right since I set foot in that room. Was it really my brother I kept seeing? My mind playing tricks? The room twisting my memories? I wanted to know. Needed to know. A distant part of me knew what I was risking. Knew that a version of this story ended with me dead, the ninth victim in a long row of unfortunate deaths. But I also knew that if I didn't face this, whatever this was, I'd be thinking about this room years from now, bound to come back looking for answers. I'd rather have my answers now. No, leaving wasn't an option. I would get to the bottom of this no matter what it took.

Layla and I headed back to our room, gently tiptoeing down the stairs so we wouldn't wake Ellis's mom. As we got closer, we could see a figure—shoulders bowed; he was bent over our door, trying to twist a knob that wouldn't give. I froze in place, sure that if he turned around, I would see my brother's face, hear his soft and quiet voice, but no—he was too tall, his hair too long. In the harsh light, I could see he had a thick beard. His black shirt was rumpled, the sleeves shoved up his arms and uneven, and he seemed panicked. Like we had caught him off guard. It was Devlin from this morning.

"Excuse me?" Layla said. I glanced down and saw our keys gripped between her fingers, ready for whatever this was.

"Sorry, sorry. I—I must have the wrong room. Good night," he said, and walked past me, his arm grazing my shoulder as he jogged a few doors down.

"Well, that was weird," she said.

Once inside, I triple-checked that the door was locked and sat down on the edge of the bed. I still felt like I was being watched though, like it was coming from somewhere inside the room. Layla grabbed a few things from her suit-case and began to head into the bathroom.

"Are you really about to take a shower?" I said. I was still thinking of all the people who had died here, three in the bathroom alone. Was I the only one fighting the urge to grab my things and run in the opposite direction of this room?

She paused for a moment, as if debating with herself, then kept walking toward the bathroom. "I need a shower after this day. The ghosts can watch," she threw back over her shoulder.

She disappeared into the bathroom, and I couldn't help but be in awe of her fearlessness. I tried distracting myself by scrolling on my phone until there were no more apps to switch to, but it wasn't working.

I moved to the desk near the bathroom door, studying the small stack of books that Layla had left there. I was surprised to see that one was about two brown girls falling in love, a YA sapphic romance with a pink cover and two hands with intricate henna designs reaching for each other. Not that it meant anything. Layla read widely. I wouldn't read into this.

I wouldn't.

After a few minutes, Layla came out of the bathroom in her pajamas, her face still wet from her shower. She stumbled into me, not realizing that I was only inches away from the door, and my hands landed on her hips to steady her. Her shorts were soft to the touch, and my right thumb grazed a sliver of skin at the edge of her shirt. She looked up at me, surprised. I couldn't help but notice the scattering of freckles on the bridge of her nose or the way her cheeks looked flushed from the hot water. She quickly glanced at my lips, and I could swear her breathing hitched. Just for a second.

"Sorry," she whispered.

I shook my head, not knowing what to say, and watched her walk away. She wound her hair in a bun and threw herself onto her bed.

I always thought she looked so pretty like this. Layla wore beautiful dresses, and her onyx hair was its own sort of magic. Plus, no one did a cat eye like she did. But there was something about seeing it all stripped away, purely Layla and nothing else. It was a kind of secret I was privy to.

"I'm sorry about what I said earlier," she said to the ceiling.

I looked at her, surprised that she would bring it up again.

"Don't be. You were being honest." And she was. I was aware that I had a habit of using people as distractions, and Layla could see that. I needed my mind to be elsewhere.

A new crush of the week usually did the trick. I knew that she wasn't slut shaming me. It was never about that. Layla was only pointing out what was happening in front of her.

"It's your life. I'm supposed to support you, not shame you, so I'm going to be sorry whether you like it or not."

"Thanks," I said, smiling into the word. We sat in the silence for a while, staring at the same water-stained spot on the ceiling. But the more I stared, the more it took shape. A face. A hand. A mouth. It was shifting before my eyes. Like trying to make sense of clouds.

"Do you see that?" I asked, pointing at the ceiling. But I knew the answer before I finished asking the question.

She squinted, trying to see something, anything, in the shape of it. "What do you see?"

"Never mind," I said, closing my eyes. I hoped that looking away would calm my heartbeat. Maybe there was nothing there. Maybe fear was a well I couldn't see the bottom of. All I knew was that I could feel the weight of this room, like a grain of sand slowly being pushed through an hourglass.

"What are you feeling right now?" She turned to me, curious, patient. I searched for the words, trying to explain this specific moment.

"You know that feeling you get after watching a scary movie, and every logical bone in your body tells you none of it was real? Obviously, there's no serial killer or little girl back from the well or brooding vampire two inches over your shoulder. There just isn't. But you can't help looking over every time. Or you're brushing your teeth and staring at the wall behind you in the mirror, sure that the second you bend over to spit, you'll come back up and there'll be a killer ghost vampire waiting for the right moment to get you. To pull you deeper, back to where it came from. Well, that. It's that feeling the second I walk into this room, and I can't leave it behind. The feeling follows me. Harder to nail down when I had made it all the way into town, but even up there in Ellis's room, it took time for me to lose the feeling. To feel like myself again. It's like a stain inside me, slowly seeping outward. I thought it was me at first, that I was going crazy. But after what Ellis told us tonight? I don't know, Layla. Nothing makes sense anymore. I want him to be right and I'm afraid of him being right."

She reached her hand out between our beds for me to squeeze. I held it and let it stay there, both of us connected by tangled fingers.

"If this was a scary movie, this would be the part where the audience asks, 'Why would they go back? They're just asking to die.' Then we die and someone throws popcorn at the screen in frustration," she said.

I wanted to laugh, revel in the lighter note for a second.

But instead, I told her, "I have to know. What this means. For me. Khalil. I don't think I'm imagining this. I don't think it's all in my head. God, I hope not. But maybe we can find answers here." I knew that I was being stubborn, that maybe I was burying the logical part of me to make room for this decision, but it didn't feel like I had a choice.

She smiled and squeezed my hand.

"Then let's do it." She let go and sat up. "I feel like a Ghostbuster. What do we do? How do we do it?"

"I guess we . . . wait?"

We sat in silence for a minute, but it felt silly, waiting for something to jump out from the shadows.

"What if we set up my camera right there," she said, pointing between our two beds to the top of the old TV. "My battery won't hold up for the whole night, but we should be okay for a while, and if we keep the lamp on, there should be enough light to catch anything that happens."

"Genius. Let's do it."

Layla grabbed her bag and prepped her camera. I dug around in my duffel and took out an old T-shirt and shorts and changed into them. I could see Layla busying herself with the camera. She messed around with the settings, trying to get everything right. Clearly, she had a valid reason for being busy, but I couldn't help but wonder if she had her back to me on purpose, forcing herself not to look at me while I changed.

She checked the display a few times, trying to get the lighting just right, and clicked record. Then she knelt in front of the camera and said, "Room 9, take one. Let's do this."

SIXTEEN

The two girls sit across from each other. They wait for a boy bathed in shadows to come crawling out of darkness, but this is not how these things go. They cannot will this to appear, cannot demand the presence of things beyond them.

The two girls turn on the TV and watch the screen. One forgets why they are here, loses herself in the laugh track. The other is impossibly aware of every shift and slight movement in the room. Every creak and draft and shape that hides just out of reach.

This fear exists in the wait, in the place between question and answer. What use would it be to give these secrets away just yet? Mira's pulse races a little faster than usual. She can feel the weighty air inside her lungs, but she takes her deep breaths. Counts to four and back again and tries to focus on the screen.

But it's no use. As long as she is here, this crushing

weight will imprint itself a little deeper onto her skin. It leaves its mark on Mira, always a little stronger than the time before.

Soon, there will be no parting with it.

SEVENTEEN

Layla

In the dim light and beneath warm covers, it felt easier to bring up what I'd wanted to avoid in the daylight. Maybe it was that static in the air, that newness of being alone in a strange place. Imagined or not, it made me braver. Mira sat still in her bed. She was looking at something in the corner of the room, a place the light couldn't reach. She looked away and focused back on the screen.

"Do you like Ellis?" I said into the quiet. Mira lowered the volume on the TV and turned to me.

"Sure, what's not to like. He seems nice. Friendly."

"No, no. I mean do you *like* like him?"

"What is this, middle school?" She chuckled but didn't answer.

"It's okay if you do, you know. I know I've been a jerk about it, but that's my problem, not yours." It wasn't news to either of us that I had been a jerk, but admitting it lifted some of the tension that found its way between us.

"What if I did? How would you feel about that?" she said.

"I just said it would be okay."

"That doesn't answer my question."

"You didn't answer mine." We both waited for the other to break first. Finally, hesitantly, I said, "I would . . . think that he'd be very lucky. To be liked by you."

Mira narrowed her eyes, sensing there was more.

"Well, I don't like him like that. We're just friends. All of us are friends. There's no reason it has to be more." She paused for a second and said, "How come you've never gone out with anyone?"

I was surprised by her question, caught off guard by her directness. "I guess I haven't liked anyone like that."

"Oh, come on. Not a single person? We know for a fact that Ben Huang liked you. You guys would have been great together. And don't think I've forgotten that Oliver Miller from book club asked you to homecoming last fall and you panicked and said you had to walk your cat that night? What was that? You don't even have a cat!"

"I have no idea! I'm allergic and I still went with that."

She sighed dramatically. "Poor Oli . . . if only he knew we stayed in and had a Keira Knightley marathon."

"Still, that was a better night than any date with Oliver."

"You don't know that. You never gave him a chance."

"I do know that. I have literally never regretted hanging out with you. What lame boy is going to change that?"

Mira smiled. "Obviously, you're not wrong. I just wish you gave other people the same chance you gave me."

"What's the point? My parents will never let me date, and it's too exhausting to have to lie all the time about where I am and who I'm with. We graduate in a few months. Dating can wait until college. Plus, it's not like our choice of high school boys makes it that hard to resist them."

"What about . . . the girls?" Mira asked softly.

She didn't want to push. I knew that. But the question looked like it fell from her mouth and shocked her on the way out. I did what I did best. Evade.

"What about them? You know my family. Can you even imagine how they'd react if I brought a girl home? Hi, Mom and Dad. This is my girlfriend. Can she stay for dinner?" I laughed at the image. "They would throw us both out."

My heart sped up at my own words. It felt thrilling to say it. To let it be real for a single sentence before it disappeared again.

Us.

She looked up at the word *us*. Not that I meant her. But it sounded like I did for a second. Of course, I sort of did. I wasn't thinking about other girls the way I thought about her. Sure, I'd had other crushes. Sarah Johnson last year, or

Lizzie Bates in National Honor Society. I liked them, but it never meant anything. Whatever I had felt faded after a while. Not like with Mira. But she didn't need to know how much I meant it, how much I wanted her.

"Give them more credit. Maybe they'll understand. My parents were surprisingly cool when I told them I was bi."

"Your dad didn't talk to you for three months and your mom signed you up for Arabic school on the weekends, as if that was going to scare you straight. She also refuses to acknowledge it no matter how many times you bring it up."

"Exactly. Surprisingly cool."

We laughed until it was quiet again.

"Well, it's not like it matters. I'm not. Gay, I mean. I'm not gay."

"Okay," she said, letting it rest.

However fleeting it was, it was nice to pretend that I was taking her home. I'd wear that green dress of mine she loved. The one with the boat neck and deep pockets. My mom would make mulukhiyah for dinner and ka'ak for dessert, even though it wasn't Eid.

Obviously, my family had met her a million times. Mira *was* family. My sisters liked her. My parents liked that my best friend was Arab too. Not that they knew even half of Mira. Only I knew all of Mira.

I looked at her for a second. Her eyes were trained

on the TV, but it didn't seem like she was listening. She didn't even smile when the laugh track played. Mira knew. She must have, right? What I was thinking? Feeling? She must have seen through the lies that were spewing from my mouth. She must have known how I felt by now.

I knew my family could never accept something like me coming out. Seeing Mira's family's reaction didn't do anything to ease my worries. Hers came to America when they were in college. They were younger, had more time to acclimate, to let certain ideas sink in. Maybe not all the way down, but enough that certain things rested just below their surface, a part of them. It made her coming out easier to swallow.

Mine were different. Old and new ideas mixed like two seas. The divide would always exist.

Mine would be convinced it was a passing phase brought on by too much Western culture. As if this didn't exist back home in Egypt. As if this were unique to America. I couldn't hate them for it. Generations of bias and ideology are hard to do away with, with one queer daughter. And who was I kidding? I definitely was queer, if my insides after one smile from Mira were any indication. Not being allowed to date was this great excuse for not having to defend myself to Mira about why I didn't talk about boys. What use was having any sort of crush when I could do nothing about it? I would tell her. It was just truer than she ever knew.

Whatever moment this was, it had passed. I'd had a chance, my second tonight, to be more honest than I was, and I had made my decision. She raised the volume on the TV and we continued watching, the camera's red light glowing above it.

EIGHTEEN

Mira

Two feet away from me was Layla, passed out and softly snoring. I knew it wasn't the plan, and I really did try to keep her up for a little while, but she looked so cute with her mouth half-open, her black hair wrapped into a messy bun. The strands that escaped haphazardly framed her face, and I didn't have the heart to wake her. The camera was recording, and if anything happened, I'd let her know the minute it did. My phone buzzed with a text from Ellis. **Everything okay?** he said. I sent back a thumbs-up emoji and put my phone on the charger. It was nice of him to check in, though I wondered if he was relieved or disappointed I didn't have anything to report. I stood up and took Layla's phone from her hand to plug it in too. She mumbled something in her sleep and turned toward me, our faces much closer than I had expected. I gently set the phone down and pulled away.

Looking at her, I couldn't help but think of a particular

snowy day a year and a half ago. I had just come out to my parents and been met by silence made only more deafening by the winter quiet outside. I remembered that the snow was heavy on the ground and how the branches were weighed down by it all.

Neither of them could think of anything to say, and Khalil, feeling all our discomfort, grabbed the keys and said, "Mira and I are going to grab pizza for dinner. We'll be back." Beneath my building panic at their lack of a reaction, I felt a surge of affection for my little brother, who somehow always knew exactly what to do.

Before either of my parents could protest, he grabbed our coats and walked out, leaving the door open behind him. I had already come out to him a few weeks earlier, but I knew he would have jumped in and saved me from this awkwardness even if he had found out right then. I hadn't been nervous when I told him. I wanted to tell him, wanted him to know. And in true Khalil fashion, he said, "I called it," and laughed, kindly. He always seemed to know more than the rest of us.

I looked at my parents now, giving them one more chance to say something. Anything. But they just looked at the snow blowing onto our hardwood floor in the open doorway. I ached to know what they were thinking then. If I was a disappointment. If they had done something wrong.

If this was preventable. If. If. If. I knew better than to hope for more than this.

And yet.

I closed the door behind me and took a second to feel the cold air in my lungs, the snowflakes on my bare arms. Khalil threw the keys over to me and got into the passenger seat. Neither of us bothered with our coats, choosing to leave them abandoned in the back seat.

"So," he said once I'd been driving for a few minutes.

"So."

The only sound was slow tires against fresh snow.

"They seem to be handling this very well," he said in mock seriousness.

I laughed. "Is that what you would call that?"

"No, no. That didn't go over well at all. But maybe they just need time to process. I figured leaving for a little bit couldn't hurt."

"Yeah, probably not," I said as I pulled into the pizza place.

"Maybe now you and Layla . . ." He let it hang there, the words floating somewhere between us. I was glad I had parked by then, or we might have slid right into the restaurant.

"What? No. That's not— Why would you think that?" My words stumbled over one another on their way out.

He looked at me with a raised eyebrow. "I'm thirteen, not an idiot."

"Even if that was true, Layla's straight. So."

"You should tell her anyway. Or you're just going to regret it. Maybe not yet. But sooner or later, you'll wish you'd have said something. And isn't sexuality a spectrum? She should know how you feel."

I looked at him, in awe of this little kid who, as far as I knew, knew nothing of dating or love or life.

"Okay, but how are you this wise and all-knowing at thirteen?"

"It's a gift and a curse," he said, quoting the show *Monk*. Ever since our parents had made us sit through the first few episodes, it had become our feel-good show. We'd spent hours binging every episode, the whole family laughing over one another. Unaware of the grenade I would gently hand them in our quiet living room on an unassuming Saturday evening.

Khalil left to place our order and the car was silent again. I ached to call Layla, to tell her what had happened with my parents. But I also couldn't help but imagine what it would be like to tell her how I felt. Not even to ask if she felt the same. It wasn't about that. Just to give her this truth that I had kept from her for a long while now. To lay it between us, a grenade of a different sort. Acknowledging its existence would be enough.

I never did tell her. I texted her about my parents and swallowed back everything else I wanted to say, let it live in the pit of my stomach, let it bloom in that space until it grew vines inside every inch of me, wanting, pleading to be let out.

I looked back at her now, still sleeping and unaware of any feelings I held for her. And yet, how could she not know? I always felt like I was glaringly obvious around her. How I had to force myself to look away, the way my body shifted toward her in every room we were in. I was fooling myself if I thought she didn't know. In all likelihood, she knew exactly how I felt and didn't have the heart to break mine.

I checked my phone. 4:13 A.M. The plan was to stay up until morning. But we'd been here for hours and nothing had happened. I sat in bed and opened my book, my back against the headboard. I shifted, and my elbow landed on the remote, turning the TV on again.

This time, soft static seeped from the speakers. Beneath it was something else. Beneath it, I could swear, was a voice. It sounded like two frequencies tangled together. One as soft as sand and the other frantic, hurried.

Familiar.

Beneath the static was Khalil screaming for help. The memory rushed back. I blinked, and suddenly I was in the Mediterranean Sea off the coast of Tunis again.

My parents safely on the shore. Water crashing over my brother's head as he screamed for help, first in English, then in his halting Arabic when he realized no one could understand him.

I froze in place, straining to make out the same word again and again, عاوني

The ع guttural and broken, stuck in the back of his throat and shoved out to make room for the rest.

"Layla," I whispered in her direction. She didn't move. I threw the book at her and she sprang up, disoriented but alert.

"I'm awake. What is it? What happened?" she said. She looked around the room, searching for clues. I shushed her, pointed to the TV, and let myself be slightly comforted by the fact that, finally, something was happening in this room and I wasn't alone to witness it.

"The TV? Did it turn on on its own?" she whispered.

"What? No, no. Listen. Underneath the static. Don't you hear it?"

She closed her eyes and focused, trying to make it out, but after a few seconds, she opened her eyes and shook her head.

"What do you hear?" she asked.

"Khalil, screaming for help. Like he did before he . . ." I let the sentence drift. She knew where it was going.

"I'm sorry, Mira," she said. She looked heartbroken, like

it hurt her that she was the one to have to break the news to me. "I don't hear anything."

I threw my head back and stared at the water-stained ceiling. Shit. I could still hear him. That same word again and again. It was so clear. Even with the static, there was no mistaking his voice, his cry for help. I couldn't save him then, and I couldn't do shit now. Layla reached over and grabbed the remote. She shut off the TV and put the remote on the nightstand between our beds.

"Why don't we trade off? I'm up now, and I'll keep watch for the rest of the night. You get some sleep. If anything happens, I promise I'll wake you, okay?"

As much as my insides screamed against it, all I wanted was to turn on the TV and hear his voice again. I hated this. I knew what I saw, what I heard. But within seconds, my brain responded with *Do you? How can you be sure? There's nothing here after all.* And I was left with gaslighting myself into submission. Maybe I really was wrong. Maybe the deaths were all a coincidence and I was hearing what I wanted. A brother who wasn't there anymore.

"Thanks," I said, and turned away from the light, my back to her. If I was slowly going insane, then I could wait until morning to come to terms with that.

NINETEEN

Mira is right. If she turns the TV back on, she will hear her brother's voice, will be able to separate his screams from the static on instinct. But instead, Mira drifts off to sleep. Restless at first, then deep, and deeper still. She sinks into darkness and, yet again, is faced with the Pull. A sense of control is back within the room. Any walls that Mira bothered to put up are now paper thin and tenuous. The sound of her brother's voice has burrowed into her like something in search of home, has nestled into her crevices, and now Mira's confidence is waning. Hearing her brother has cracked her open. It is almost too easy to see inside her shell. She is unguarded and exposed.

It is only her and the dream and the Pull that winds its way through. For a moment, there is a disturbance outside the dream. An interruption. An interlude, if you will. The Pull being stretched in different directions. But comprehension, attention, is not a monolithic idea, and so another arm, a tentacle, a vine goes off to study the interlude.

But for now, the dream begins.

First, the darkness. The water floods in. Mira struggles to orient herself, but then the limbs come. They surround every part of her. She looks up to see that the surface is closer than she thinks, only inches away. But this unintelligible body is embracing her from above, and there is nowhere to go. Mira feels the burning in her lungs, the tightness in her throat. Can feel her pulse in the back of her eyes, pounding away. She feels she will explode into herself.

Her fingers grab at the face above the surface and this time, the face looks back. Even through the frantic rushing of the water, she can make out the features, the wet tumbled hair, the large hazel eyes. There is no mistaking the scar at the edge of her jaw.

It is Mira looking back from above. She is unflinching and she is calm.

For a single slow second, Mira is both drowner and drowning.

The image then reverses. Our Mira is now above the surface, her arms and legs wrapped around a body beneath the water. The face beneath is different now, blurred.

Thrashing.

Panicked.

Every piece of her knows it is Khalil trapped underneath. She wants to let go. Wants to set him free. But he is like a body beneath ice, and she is solid and frigid and unmovable around him. Their eyes meet, and as fleeting as it is, the moment sears itself into a place she can never reach. How can she forget him now when his final moment is imprinted inside of her somewhere?

She wakes and she doesn't.

Her eyes spring open, but her body is still frozen inside the dream. She feels arms around her trying to pull her back in, gripping her shoulders. If she looks down, she is convinced she will see them. The shapes of fingers, hands bent at the wrists, rigid and everywhere. But she can't look down. Mira can only stare at the water-stained ceiling as frantic hands grasp for the safety they think they will find on her body.

TWENTY

Layla

"Mira? You awake?" I must have nodded off. When I woke up, I could see that her eyes were wide open but she wasn't moving. She just lay there, frozen. I stood up and leaned over, trying to make sure she was okay. Her eyes met mine. They looked frantic, panicked. She glanced down, but her body was rigid, as if every stiff muscle refused to yield to her.

"Mira? Mira. Can you hear me?" I shook her gently, trying to wake her, but she was frozen in place as if bolted to the bed. I sat down at the edge of her bed and waited. Her fingers tightened around my hand for a second, and slowly, finally, she came to.

"Hey, you're okay. I'm here."

She sat up when her body let her and stretched like she was testing the limits of limbs.

"I don't know what the hell that was," she said.

"Sleep paralysis, I think? My mom used to get it. Like

you're stuck between awake and asleep. Your body just takes a little while to catch up to the fact that you've woken up. Has it happened before?"

She shook her head and hugged her knees to her chest. "This felt— I don't know if it was that. It felt so real. Like I was drowning, like something wanted to pull me back into the water even when I woke up. I could feel hands on me, pulling me under."

"It happens. The brain doesn't know what's real in those moments. Only ever lasts for a few minutes at best. You're okay, I promise." I smiled, trying to reassure her, but she still looked scared.

"I think I need to go for a run or something."

"Now? It's six in the morning. It's barely light out."

"Yeah, I need some air," she said. She threw her covers back and started changing into an oversized T-shirt and leggings. I started to look away, but she was done in two seconds.

"Want company? Can't promise I can keep up, but I can promise I'll jog a few feet behind you, out of breath."

"It's okay. I'll be back soon."

With that, she slammed the door behind her. I wished I knew how to help her, but neither of us knew what this was. Maybe it was the room. I didn't want to believe that she was hearing and seeing things. I really had tried to approach last night with an open mind. But there was nothing beneath the

176 | A GUIDE TO THE DARK

static, and sleep paralysis, as scary as it is, is pretty normal. Really, it was Ellis's fault for filling our heads with conspiracy theories. People die. It's what they do. And now he had Mira doubting her own sanity because he couldn't accept the fact that his dad killed himself. I fell back into bed and closed my eyes. Maybe I also hated how much attention he paid Mira, how it made me feel like a side character in whatever supernatural story they were writing. But that was beside the point. There was nothing I could do for either of them. I felt relief knowing that we would be gone by tomorrow morning. That this entire place would be behind us. What an odd intermission it had been.

I was too awake to sleep now. I turned on the TV. The channel was still set to static. Before I could convince myself to change the channel, I gave it one more chance. I strained to listen, trying to make out anything underneath the noise, but it was just more static. I couldn't hear what Mira heard. I flipped the channels until I settled on something and watched it mindlessly for a while. Mostly I just wanted to sleep, but sleep didn't want me.

My phone buzzed on the nightstand. Before I could answer, a text popped up from Mouna in my sister group chat.

A letter came for you from a school in Chicago. Mom is pissed. Just a heads-up that she's about to call you.

Fuck.

"Hello?" I greeted her in Arabic.

"Is there anything you want to tell me?" was all she said.

I considered lying, stretching it out, but what was the point? We'd end up in the same place. "You got a letter from a school I applied to in Chicago?"

Silence.

"Well, yes. I— How did you know?"

"Wild guess."

More silence.

"What does the letter say?" It was almost a whisper. I was afraid of the answer.

"You're off the waitlist. You got in."

I wanted to scream. I wanted to throw my phone across the room and dance until my legs gave out.

Somehow, "Oh?" was all I said.

"SAIC isn't even offering you any scholarships. You can't actually be thinking of going. You've been accepted to the University of Michigan. You can do your photography hobby on the side. We talked about this."

"I just needed to know if I could get in. It's a great photography program, that's all." I could imagine her raised eyebrow, her pursed lips. I wasn't sure if she believed me. I didn't believe me. I wanted this so badly. And yet.

"I won't tell your dad. He'll be too upset about this. But

we'll talk about this when you get home." I knew she meant it as a threat, a *Be grateful I'm the only one who knows about this*, but sometimes I felt like my dad would be the one to understand this more than she ever would. Like maybe he seemed so firmly on her side out of obligation, not conviction. He knew what it was like to leave home, to travel alone and know that the world was more than the bubble you were born into. I wished he was the one who'd found the letter. Maybe then I wouldn't have to wonder.

"Okay."

As soon as she hung up, I could feel my excitement withering. Could I really go to school in Chicago when my parents expected me to stay so close to home? Or when I had a scholarship at Parsons? New York could be great. It was far from family and Mira and everything I knew, but it was New York. Still, my heart wasn't there. My heart would be a few miles away from SAIC, going to her own classes at the University of Chicago.

An hour later, Mira came back. Her curls were matted to her forehead. Her cheeks were red, and she was out of breath. I could see sweat trickling down her neck and disappearing inside her shirt. She took a few seconds to breathe before she spoke.

"Just texted Ellis. Told him to meet us at the diner. Want to come with me to check on the car first?" she said.

"Sure, let me get dressed."

She nodded, took a few things from her duffel, and then paused. I watched as she squared her shoulders, took a deep breath, and headed into the bathroom. I wanted to tell her my good news. Or conflicting news. Or whatever it was. But she seemed preoccupied, worried about this room and how she felt in it. One crisis at a time. My news could wait. I grabbed a dark red cotton summer dress with thin straps that tied into bows at the shoulders. It was a little early in the year for it, the air still chilly, but I was eager to wear it. The top half hugged my chest while the skirt flared out into loose and light fabric. It was one I'd found at a thrift store a few days ago when we were in New York. God, it felt like months ago I was walking through aisles looking at pretty clothes. Now I was getting dressed to tell a boy there were no ghosts in his haunted room.

"Ready?" Mira asked as she walked out of the bathroom a minute later. She was wearing an olive-green jumpsuit and was in the process of tying it at the waist. Her hair was wet, but I hadn't even heard the shower.

"That was fast."

"Yeah, rinsed off in the sink. We're running late. Didn't want to keep Ellis waiting." Mira avoided my eyes, looking everywhere but at me, but I knew a Mira lie when I heard one. She burrowed through her duffel for a second and took out her curl cream. I watched as she squeezed a dollop into her palm and scrunched it into her wet hair. I barely had time to put on mascara before she was at the door sliding into her brown heeled Timberland boots. I looked at the six pairs of shoes I had packed. Three flats in an assortment of colors, one pair of white Adidas sneakers with the classic black stripes down the sides, brown sandals with white ribbons that wrapped around my calf, and heels I'd yet to wear on this trip. I envied Mira's quick choice in footwear, considering it was either sneakers, boots, or combats, and slipped my feet into the Adidas. I grabbed my camera from on top of the TV and quickly replaced the battery before turning my attention back to the dress.

"Wait, can you help me with the straps?" I asked her. "I can't tie them myself."

I could tell she was impatient, ready to leave as her hand toyed with the doorknob back and forth, but she paused when I asked her and glanced at my bare shoulders. She walked over to me and stood so close, I could feel the heat of her. The scent of lavender and fresh linen wafted between us, and I wanted to close my eyes and let it envelop me. Her hands found the straps for my right shoulder and she wound them together into loops. The feel of her fingertips against my bare skin left my heart beating noticeably faster.

I wondered if she could hear it, the rattling of my rib cage around quick heartbeats.

She turned her attention to my left shoulder, and where her hands softly brushed against my skin felt like a flame, the tips of her fingers flickering between fabric and skin. Mira was a little taller than me, so I kept my eyes trained on her collarbones peeking out of the edge of her jumpsuit, almost afraid to look at her face, to see whatever expression lay there, to see if it was as obvious as mine. Finally, she stepped back, admiring the delicate bows at my shoulders, and smiled. I grabbed my camera, and we headed out.

We started walking to the mechanic, but it was beginning to feel like a jog with the pace Mira was setting. It was warmer today, and even though it was April, I could feel sweat dripping down my chest and back. I opened the door to the mechanic and reveled in the cold air that came rushing out.

"Hello, ladies, what can I do for you?" the man behind the counter said.

"We spoke yesterday; you have my car, the 2004 Chrysler Sebring. I just wanted to check in and make sure it was going to be ready to go tomorrow."

"Sure thing. Should be ready by then. We replaced your windshield and rim, and someone's working on the front axle. Just waiting on the new airbags to come in since they deployed, so call or come by tomorrow and you can pick it up then."

Mira seemed to release whatever breath she was holding.

"Great, I'll see you then," she said.

Mira led the way to the diner a few buildings down. We sat down in a booth near the back. She studied the menu like she was about to be quizzed on it. She looked tired, bags under her eyes from not having slept well for two days now. I wished I could help, but there wasn't anything for me to do but sit across from her.

"You okay?" I said. She nodded but didn't look up. Just continued staring at the menu between us.

"I didn't think we'd be meeting this early. It's not even eight. Why would you guys do this to me?" Ellis said when he reached our table. He looked a little rumpled in his brown shirt and dark corduroy pants. Mira scooted deeper into her side of the booth to make room for him.

"Aren't you curious about what happened last night?" I said. That woke him up a little.

"Did something happen?" he whispered. He looked back and forth at us, waiting for an answer. Mira shook her head as the same waiter from yesterday made his way over.

"What can I get you?"

"Pancakes. Thanks, man," Ellis said.

I didn't want to get the same thing as Ellis. I really didn't. But damn it, I wanted pancakes.

"Make that two stacks," I said.

The boy with the buzz cut looked at Mira, waiting for her order, but she sat there frozen, her eyes locked on his hands, his fingers wrapped around a pen.

"Mira?" I said.

"Garden omelet." She hurriedly folded up her menu and set it at the center of the table, making sure not to look at the boy taking the order. It wasn't what I would have guessed she would order after staring at the menu for five minutes, but okay.

The waiter wrote it all down and made his way back to the kitchen.

"Okay. So, what happened?" Ellis asked once he was out of earshot.

"Nothing. I . . . I thought I heard something," Mira finally said. "My brother screaming for help in Arabic beneath the static of a channel on the TV. Like he did when he drowned. But Layla didn't hear anything, so I don't know what to tell you."

I pulled out my camera and played back the video we had made last night. It was still recording at that point, so at least now, we could play it back and listen for it. If there was proof to be had, it would be here. They both shifted toward the wall and made room for me to come sit on their side.

I moved over and clicked play. It was odd seeing Mira and me sitting in our beds watching TV. Unsettling. Like we were being watched and were only now realizing it. The Layla on the screen laughed at something on TV while Mira sat there, her face still and stoic. She looked around the room, waiting for something. I looked so oblivious to her unease. Where was I really? A few seconds in and I remembered this video was at least four hours long. I went to fast-forward to the end, but not before Ellis heard me ask the Mira on my camera if she liked Ellis. I don't think I've clicked anything faster. Ellis didn't comment, most likely pretending that he didn't hear it. But his body grew stiff next to mine, and I noticed the glance he stole at Mira. Only a second, barely anything, but all of us knew he heard it. And now he would never hear her answer. I basked in the fact that he'd always wonder what she said to that.

Finally, at the four hour and seven minute mark, the Mira on-screen shifted and accidentally turned on the TV. She sat up, intent on listening to what was beneath the shushing static that filled the room, and now the booth. On-screen Mira tried to get my attention, threw a book in my direction; I woke up, told her I didn't hear anything. I had hoped that I was wrong, that now, as we played back the video, I would hear what Mira heard, but all I heard was static.

"Do you hear anything?" I asked Ellis. He took the camera and rewound a few seconds, to when it was clear Mira could hear the voice. He held the camera up to his ear, searching for any ounce of proof. But after a few seconds, he set it back down and shook his head.

"Right now, I don't hear it either," Mira said. "I don't know why I could last night and not now, but whatever it was, it's not there."

"Did anything else happen?" he asked.

"I had a bad dream? I couldn't move when I woke up. I could feel hands all over me pulling me down. But it was probably sleep paralysis. Stress or something," she said.

"Can we look at that part of the video? Maybe there's something more to that that the camera caught," Ellis said. We could hear the edge in his voice, desperate for a sign that the room was more than it was. We had no plan B.

I clicked play and began fast-forwarding.

All of us froze when we saw the figure flash across the screen.

I wound it back and let it play.

There was the soft click of the door unlocking. Then the shape of a man walking past the camera. He was all shadows in the low light, no way to make out his features, but he was very much there. He reappeared in frame a few seconds later and paused, unmoving as he faced the camera. He was too close to the lens; only his torso was visible. He rummaged through the large dresser the TV rested on. Sleeping me mumbled something. *Mira*, it sounded like, and my cheeks flushed knowing they both heard it. The figure froze as the seconds on the time stamp ticked by.

Five.

Ten.

Fifteen.

Eventually, he walked toward the nightstand between our beds. In the lamplight he was a silhouette burrowing through the drawer, looking for something. When he didn't seem to find it, he quietly, softly turned back and looked ahead. Even then, while he looked straight at the camera, it was impossible to make out his face. He didn't seem to realize the camera was recording. He just stared, lost in thought. After a few seconds, he walked around Mira's bed and left the frame. Video me woke up at the sound of the door shutting behind him.

"Holy shit," Ellis said.

I moved back to my side of the booth and stared at my camera.

"What the hell did we just see? Who would break into our room? He didn't even take anything. He just stood there for the longest time before he even looked," Mira said. She was getting loud and high-pitched, terrified at the thought of what could have happened. We both were.

At the sound of the bell at the door, I looked up to see a man wearing a baseball cap walk in and take a seat at a table near the register. It was the same man from outside our room last night, the one who mumbled *Wrong room* and rushed past us. In broad daylight, with his features well lit, he felt familiar. I hadn't pieced it together last night, but then I knew. I looked back at my camera, hoping I was wrong.

I flipped through the photos we had taken on this trip. He was harder to make out at first, but there he was.

In all of them.

In the shots I took while I waited for Mira by the pool.

Following Mira and Ellis as we walked to town.

Out of focus, in a shot of Mira at the bookstore.

Again and again.

And now at a table a few feet away from us. I would bet anything he had been the man in our room.

TWENTY-ONE

Mira

"It's a small town. Basically made up of two blocks and an intersection. Maybe it's a coincidence?" Ellis said.

The waiter came back with our food, and this time his hands didn't look like my brother's. They looked like his own. Chewed-up nails, a phone number quickly scrawled at his wrist. It was still hard to breathe, but now at least my shoulders could relax. We all stopped talking until he left again. I didn't have the stomach for breakfast anymore.

"No way. This is too weird. Do you see this?" Layla turned the camera toward us and flipped through the pictures again, hitting the button harder each time for emphasis. I took the camera from her and my fingers brushed her hand. It was quick, a passing moment if anything at all, but I looked up and knew I wasn't imagining the creeping blush in her cheeks. The camera was warm where she had held it.

"He was outside our room too, trying to open the door

when we walked up to him," she said a little too quickly. "He mumbled something about having the wrong room and ran off. It has to be him."

I wondered how he got into the room and then I realized. It must have been when his arm grazed my shoulder. My keys were in my pocket. How could I not have noticed his hand creeping into my pocket?

"His name is Devlin. I met him yesterday on my run. He seemed fine, maybe a little strange, but definitely didn't think he'd end up breaking into our room."

"What the fuck? Has he been watching us since we got here?" Layla said. She was frowning into her pancakes, her hands in tight fists around the fork and knife.

"What do you think he wants?" Ellis said.

"Let's find out," I said. I was tired of feeling helpless. Of having weird thing after weird thing happen to me. I didn't know why I was seeing things or hearing things or why I felt so damn heavy and anxious in that room. I didn't know why a strange man would break in, in the middle of the night, and take nothing. But I sure as hell could find out. I motioned for Ellis to move, and for a second, he looked scared. I'd known him for a day, and I could already tell Ellis and confrontation did not mix. He stood up, stumbling over his feet for a second.

"Coming?" I said to Layla. She smiled at me, ready for

whatever was about to happen next. They both followed me to the man's table—Ellis begrudgingly, Layla eagerly.

Devlin looked up as we approached. He didn't try to hide the surprise on his face, his eyes jumping from one of us to the next as he straightened up and swallowed. I sat down in the empty chair in front of him but didn't say anything just yet. Layla pulled out the chair at a neighboring table to my right, and Ellis stood over both of us awkwardly, unsure of what to do with his hands.

"We know you were in our room last night, and we know you've been following us," I said. "Unless you want us to call the cops, I suggest you tell us what you want and why you're here."

"Speak for yourself. We might call the cops anyway, pervert," Layla added.

"I—hello, um, I'm Devlin Gallagher," he said to the others. "I'm sorry. I shouldn't have gone in there when you both were sleeping. I mean, I shouldn't have gone in there at all! I just—I can't explain it. It was like the room was calling, whispering. I needed to go inside. I needed to find something. Anything."

"You were the guy in the parking lot, watching our window two nights ago, weren't you?" I said. Looking at him was like filling in the silhouette of his shoulders and hair against the light. It had to be.

He opened his mouth to defend himself but closed it and nodded. There was no excuse.

"Oh my God. You've been following us since the night we got here?" Layla couldn't hide the look of disgust on her face if she tried. Not that she wanted to. "Why? Why the hell would you do that?"

Ellis, in a kinder voice, said, "Why that room?"

"My wife stayed in that room, and I—I needed answers."

The three of us looked at one another, wondering the same thing.

"What was her name?" Ellis said from behind us.

"Maddie. Madeline Gallagher."

We looked back at Ellis, but he shook his head. She wasn't one of the eight. Ellis grabbed an empty chair from a few tables over and scooted in on my left.

"Okay. We're listening," Ellis said.

Devlin looked at all of us, as if surprised that we were willing to hear him out, that it would be this easy. But he wasn't the only one with questions.

"What do you want to know?" he asked.

"What happened to your wife? Why are you here? What answers are you looking for?" Ellis said.

"Also still unclear on why you've been following us," Layla chimed in. Devlin pushed his coffee away and rested his palms on the table.

"My wife is currently in a psychiatric hospital a few miles outside Chicago. She's been there since she came back from the Wildwood Motel three months ago. We had . . .

We—" He paused, hesitant. But he cleared his throat and continued.

"A year ago, our son died. He was only two months old. When Maddie came back from the motel a few months ago, she quickly spiraled. She—she wasn't herself. She'd always hear him crying. I'd find her late at night in the nursery, pretending to rock him to sleep, her arms bent at the shape of him. She'd pull her hair out in clumps and not even know she was doing it. Then one day, we were driving home and she just opened the car door and jumped out before I even realized what was happening.

"The doctors think it's some delayed response, an inability to process what happened, some sort of psychosis. But when she's not muttering our son's name again and again, she whispers about the watching room, Room 9, and how she could feel its presence like a living thing. Some days she's convinced she's still here. I can't help her. I don't know how to. I thought that maybe if I came here, I could find something. I could . . . I don't know."

"You could understand," Ellis said. He was looking for the same answers.

"Yeah," Devlin said. "Anyway. I came here a few days ago, but someone was already in Room 9. I thought I'd wait until they left to switch rooms, to see for myself. But the day the guest checked out, you two booked it before I had the chance. I followed you yesterday, hoping you might know something, that you might have seen or felt something, that I might overhear you talking about the watching room. Maybe I should have just approached you and asked, but I didn't think you'd talk to a strange man asking stranger questions, and following you around town wasn't all that helpful in the end. So, I snuck in—"

"Broke in," Layla corrected him.

"Broke in and tried to look for answers myself. Anything that might explain what's happening to Maddie. I was going to return the key today, I swear, to tell you I had found it on the ground. I really am sorry." He took out the key from his pocket and slid it over to me.

For what it was worth, he looked like he meant it. I slipped the key into my pocket. I wasn't sure what to do with any of that information. None of us were. He straightened the salt and pepper on the table, waiting for one of us to say something.

"There's others," Ellis whispered to himself. He was staring at the table, connecting his own dots. "Excuse us."

His chair scraped against the hardwood as he hastily stood up. Layla and I followed him back to our table. Our food had gone cold. Not that it mattered. I still didn't have the stomach to even touch my omelet. Layla, on the other hand, doused her stack in maple syrup and cut a triangle out of it. Both of us stared at her as she brought it to her mouth.

"What?" she said around a bite of pancake.

"How can you eat right now?" I said.

"Easy. I'm hungry. That's how it works." She cut another piece out.

"Okay. Focus. This is— I don't know why I didn't think of it before," Ellis said. "This is incredible. I mean, not incredible. Oh, you know what I mean. It's not just the eight who died. If Madeline being in a mental hospital is connected to Room 9, then there have to be others like her, right? This could be the piece we've been missing. What we needed to know to find the pattern, to under-stand what happens in that room and how it happens," Ellis said in one big breath. He took a second and contin-ued. "We need to decide. We are at a dead end with our own attempt. Nothing strange or unexplainable made it onto the video. Layla, you didn't hear what Mira heard. And maybe that's because there's nothing to hear." He took a deep breath.

"Or maybe there's something else going on and, Mira, you're not crazy or processing your grief or whatever bull-shit I'm sure you're trying to convince yourself of right now. Maybe what your gut is telling you is that you need to listen to it."

Every part of me wanted to believe him. To trust that this was bigger than me, than my grief.

"Why should we even trust him?" Layla said. "We don't know this guy. He could be a serial killer trying to get us to fall into his trap, for all we know."

"I'm not sure. There's got to be an easier way to murder us than making up a story about an institutionalized wife and a mysterious room. Plus, if he was going to do anything, he would have done it in said room last night," I said. "I trust him. Or his story, anyway."

"All right, then I say we follow where this thread leads," Ellis said.

Layla looked at us both, her cheeks full of pancake. "I don't like it, but I'm clearly outnumbered. So sure. Why the hell not?" she said with an eye roll and a mouthful.

Ellis stood up, and we followed him back to Devlin's table. He looked a little nervous to see us again. Which was fair. This could be his dead end. But it wasn't. We all wanted the same thing.

"My name is Ellis," he said when he sat back down. He motioned over his shoulder. "This is Layla, and you know Mira. I think we can help each other."

TWENTY-TWO

The room is empty, but fear lingers like a pulse.

It wafts in the air, a feeling that rests on this old wall-paper atop years of deserted emotions. Mira's fear, her anxiety, the death that follows her, it becomes the fabric of this place. The walls, the floors, the spaces between them, they drink it all in. They lick it clean, and when they're done, they salivate for what's to come. The room waits for more.

There is always more.

TWENTY-THREE

Layla

Ellis wasted no time before diving in. Minutes into meeting this guy and Ellis was sharing all his research.

"First thing to note is you're right. Room 9 has a long and dark history, and we're only now realizing that it's much darker than the eight people who died in it."

"I read about that," Devlin said. "But the articles didn't list what room, just that people died at the Wildwood Motel."

"It's definitely Room 9. All eight stayed there, and the other rooms are incredibly uneventful in comparison. I've found no links or patterns between length of stay, gender, age, or race. They all die in very different ways, and not all are violent or gruesome. The deaths do happen closer and closer together in a forty-year time period, but again, that's the only pattern we can find.

"But Madeline. Your Madeline changes everything. Death could be the tip of the iceberg. I've spent months looking at the eight. Somehow, I thought that was the extent of it. It isn't. If what you're saying is true, if you're right, that what's happening to Madeline is linked to Room 9, then there have to be others like her over the years. Our pool of data could turn into a lake."

"What can I do?" Devlin asked.

"Help us stop the room," Ellis said. "There has to be a way, a weakness, anything, that we can target. Something we can do so that this never happens again."

"Ellis, you guys keep a record of everyone who's stayed at the motel, right?" Mira asked. "We could research all the past guests and try to find out what happened to them, see if staying in that room has affected anyone else? If there's a pattern, it would be easier to find with more people."

"Yes, yes, that's perfect," he said, pointing at her. "Then maybe we can find some sort of explanation, some answer, something to make it all make sense. To put an end to it. It's out there. We just have to find it." He stood up, eager to get started.

"I can grab our old records. We can try to see what we can dig up from past guests who haven't died in that room. Some are online, but we only went digital in the last few years. Before that, people signed a book. We still have the books in storage."

His excitement was palpable. Even Mira, who I knew

was trying to restrain herself, to not get her hopes up, to stay reasonable and clearheaded, was moving her weight from foot to foot. I swallowed down whatever reluctance I had about getting on board and got on board. At least until we left Wildwood tomorrow morning. If we were going to pull at this thread, we might as well see what was at the end of it.

TWENTY-FOUR

Mira

We all walked down the empty road and back to the motel. Ellis was filling in Devlin on everything he'd told us yesterday, going through each of the eight deaths. By now he had memorized everything on that door. But he took the time to form whatever picture he could around the details he found. A lot of this was clearly speculation, but it was nice to see the care he attempted to give the dead.

"What do you think we'll find out?" Layla asked. She was watching the video again, fast-forwarding through the rest to make sure we hadn't missed anything else.

"Maybe nothing. Maybe everything." I could tell she was trying her best to believe both me and her own logic. I appreciated the effort.

"I hope it's the latter," she said, looking up at me. We both smiled sad sorts of smiles, an acknowledgment of how odd this whole trip had been, to put it lightly, and continued. She pulled out her lens cap to click it back into place, and it slipped from her fingers, landing between our shoes. I bent down to pick it up, but so did she. When our hands met, we both paused. Frozen in place. She looked up at me, waiting for me to let go or to say something, anything, but I was out of words. I just stared back at her doe eyes and let time rush past us, stealing this tiny moment for myself. My thumb grazed hers, and it was like my fingers were moving on their own, a quick caress of her hand before I could stop them. She didn't look away this time, even when I yanked my hand back afterward.

Finally, I stood up and jogged back a few steps. She smiled and started changing the settings on her camera, trying to get the light just right. I was too in my head, so lost in the idea of what we could be that I couldn't see what was in front of me. I couldn't keep overthinking each moment, couldn't let my biased perspective color every minute I had with her. She loved me. But it would never be in the way I loved her, and I needed to figure out how to accept that. She disappeared around the corner and I knew she was waiting for me to walk into frame. After a few test shots, she was in the zone, Room 9 only a memory. Which was for the best. We were about to spend the rest of the day deep in its history. I felt bad that I was dragging her into the middle of this. She shouldn't have to be here, shouldn't have to think about the room or all it was capable of.

If it was possible to grant her a moment where she could lose herself behind her camera and the light and the framing, then how could I not give her that? She squatted low on the ground, trying to aim the camera up toward me, and quickly adjusted her settings again. Her hair fell in front of her face and she whipped it back to see through the viewfinder. I gave her my best serious model face and tipped my chin up, my eyes trained on her.

She stood and flipped over the camera to show me her favorite shot. It was beautiful, the way she framed it, but as she flipped through the photos, one thing appeared in all of them.

"What is that?" I asked, pointing at the space around me. It looked odd, out of place, like there was something near me or around me in every shot, vibrating. The way the end of a road looked in the summer heat. "Is something wrong with the camera?"

"It's in most of them. I think it's the lens. It might have taken a bigger hit than we realized that night. I only brought the one lens on the trip, and recalibrating it might help, but I haven't done that or done a deep clean on it since I got it. Not about to tear it open in that dingy motel room to figure it out."

"Are you sure it's that?" Something about this was off, unnatural. I must have been so focused on Devlin appearing

in the photos earlier that I didn't notice what now seemed so glaring. I scrolled back, looking for yesterday's pictures. Same thing. A distortion that seemed to be getting stronger, closer. Lenses didn't work like this, did they? When I moved, the warping followed.

"Either that or it's broken, so I'm not even going to think about the alternative at the moment. But," she said, excited this time, "whatever is wrong with the lens is kind of working with these photos. Doesn't it look cool?" She flipped to one she especially liked, and I nodded. She might have been right, but I just felt cold looking at it. She put the camera away, and we walked back in silence the rest of the way.

By the time we got back, we had a plan. We'd all get our laptops, Ellis would get the records, and this weird quartet would head to the library, where we would spend the day researching. We weren't sure what we were looking for, but we hoped we'd know it when we found it.

Devlin coming into the mix felt important. The odds of him being here the same week we were; that we had befriended Ellis; that he chose to be honest about what was happening in that room. It all felt fated somehow. Like we were all heading toward something bigger than us. We were supposed to head home as soon as the car was fixed, but if we said the car wasn't ready, that it would need more time, then we didn't have to leave tomorrow. Maybe it would be worth staying a few extra days, just to see this through a little more. Leaving felt wrong, especially now that we'd been given this lead.

We reached the motel and Devlin went to his room. Ellis went into the front-desk area to get his laptop and records. Layla was a few steps ahead of me, unlocking our door. I could feel it already, its looming presence. Like it had begun to seep out beneath the door and around its hinges the second she turned the key.

"Can you grab my backpack? My laptop's inside. I just—I'd rather not."

She nodded at me and smiled, but I could see it in her eyes. How she felt bad that I had to ask, that I was afraid to go inside our own motel room. I knew she was finding all of this hard to believe. I was having a hard time processing it myself. None of us knew how to define this, but we were nearing dangerously close to the supernatural. All that mattered was that I knew she was willing to hear me out, to see this through, and that was enough for me.

She came out a minute later with both our bags.

"Are you still a sister now that you have a dead brother?" she said.

I froze, unsure of what to do with that.

"I just wondered what someone did with the title of

sister when their only brother drowns." She stared at me, unblinking.

"What did you say?"

"I didn't say anything," she said. She had her hand out, waiting for me to take my bag. "Are you okay?"

I blinked and the moment was gone. I wanted to shake myself into sanity. Wanted to know when reality was twisting itself into something I couldn't recognize. But I didn't know what the hell that was, and Layla had no idea anything had even happened.

I nodded at her and slung my bag over a shoulder. I could see that she was still looking at me, concerned. But if I explained, she would have thought I was crazier than she already thought I was. All I knew was that what was happening to me was not bound by the walls of that room anymore. Little by little, the room was making its way out.

I needed to focus. I needed to learn everything about this place. If I could understand, maybe I wouldn't be scared anymore. Maybe I'd know how to make it all stop. Maybe I could stop seeing Khalil in every stranger.

As I went to open the office door, Ellis came rushing out, taking us both by the arms a few feet away, out of sight of the front desk, where his mom sat trying to get a good look at us.

"My mom can't know I'm taking the records," he

whispered. "She hates it every time I talk about the room, and she's going to find a way to stop me. I need you guys to distract her while I go in the back and grab the books. Okay?"

He didn't wait for us to agree. He just squeezed both our arms as good luck and turned back around, disappearing into the office.

"Damn it, Ellis," Layla muttered under her breath. I turned to her to see if we had a game plan, but she was closer than I thought, and I found myself looking down at her pouted lips. She seemed annoyed and adorable, and I had to force myself to take a step back before she noticed that I was having a hard time looking away from her mouth. Why did she have to be so damn pretty all the time?

Layla was still focused on where Ellis had gone. She rolled her eyes and trudged forward, ready to figure this out right then and there.

"Elena, hi. My name is Layla, by the way. This is Mira," she said, using our American pronunciations. An American *L* almost stumbles its way out of your mouth, heavy on the tongue. An Arabic ل is music. My ر was thick and rolled instead of the soft, round *R* it was here. White people usually didn't know what to do with sounds they weren't accustomed to. I always hated that everyone pronounced Khalil with that hard *K*, when really a true *K*, an Arabic ك, is deep, firm, guttural almost. It lives in the back of your throat and tumbles into the rest.

"We have a whole day left in your wonderful town, and we were wondering if you could recommend anything for us to do."

Elena looked at us with suspicion, her eyes narrowing before she decided to answer. I thought we were being smooth, but maybe she already suspected we were all up to something.

"Sure, there's a few pamphlets here. It's a small town, but it has a lot to offer." She walked over to the other side of the desk and started flipping for the one she was looking for.

Over her shoulder, Ellis stuck his head out of the open doorway, checking that everything was going fine. He disappeared again. I walked away from Layla and Elena, pretending to look at the picture frames on the far wall, and could see him stuffing two huge record books into his backpack. Clearly, it wasn't working; he barely had one in there, and his bag looked like it was ready to tear at the seams. I bent down, pretending to tie my shoelaces, and slid my bag, empty save for my laptop, across the floor and into the back room. It disappeared into the doorway just in time for his mom to look over at me.

"What about this one? Is the—" Layla paused, reading

a pamphlet at random—"bowling alley far from here?" I could see Layla attempting to hide the grimace on her face. His mom turned back around, and we were safe for another moment. Ellis went for the bag, but one of the books slipped and landed with a thud. Elena whipped around at the sound, and Layla and I froze.

"Can I take your picture?" Layla asked a little too loudly. "The light's just right. I'd love to get a portrait."

"Sure," she said, blushing. Her hands fluttered in front of her, unsure of what to do with themselves until she settled with placing them flat on the desk.

Ellis, crouched low to the ground, smiled at me, wide and full of teeth. He stuffed the second book into my backpack and walked out, placing it near my feet just as his mom turned around. Layla clicked. The sound caught Elena's attention again and she faced Layla this time, letting her get the shot.

"The bowling alley? I can walk you guys there. It's on my way to the library," Ellis said as he headed out of the office. Elena started to protest, her mouth already forming the *El* in *Ellis*, but she stopped and waved goodbye.

"Thanks for the photo!" Layla yelled out as she caught up with Ellis. I picked up my bag, now one large book heavier, and followed them out.

TWENTY-FIVE

They come back. The scent of Ellis wafts in for a fleeting moment, and it disappears too quickly. Ellis, who for months has been just out of reach, as if forever resting where the sun meets the road. But he is flickering, shimmering, wavering to the Pull. He disappears, and Mira faces the room. This time, she is too afraid to step inside. She waits, lets what she needs come to her, places both feet firmly on the ground, inches from the doorway. She is pulling herself back, but it is foolish to think her precautions have any bearing on reality.

On Mira's reality.

It's fun, lulling Mira into this false sense of safety, letting her believe she can escape if only she keeps her distance. But the thread that binds her here is longer than she knows, stronger than she thinks.

When Mira's friend comes out of the room, she says, "Are you still a sister now that you have a dead brother?"

The words take over the girl. She is more message than girl now. Oblivious. Obedient.

The fear, the panic, the pain that rise from Mira are palpable. The room absorbs them in one big gulp.

The friend continues. "I just wondered what someone did with the title of sister when their only brother drowns."

Mira is speechless at this turn of events, unsure of what to feel aside from this pain. But the moment is brief, sufficient. There is no need to drag it out.

Mira understands.

TWENTY-SIX
Layla

This library was beautiful. For a small town in the middle of nowhere, I guess it made sense that their library felt like an escape. The ceilings were high, and wide windows lit up the space. Tables ran down the center with rows of books surrounding them, all neatly shelved and waiting for me to run down the aisles, my fingers skimming every spine. I snapped a few photos, even though I knew they wouldn't do this place justice. There wasn't any warping here. But as interesting as they would have looked, I wondered if Mira was onto something, if the distortions that always seemed to surround her were more than a trick of the light or a faulty lens. I had brushed it off this whole time. Had focused on what it could be, a boost for my portfolio. But maybe I was just selfish, oblivious to what this place was trying to tell us. Either way, I didn't have those answers.

On each table were two lamps, the kind with curved green glass I had always wanted. The sound of typing and

turning pages softly echoed. There were a few people scattered across the large space, but it was deserted for the most part. We followed Ellis as he made his way toward a table in the back.

"Elly," someone whisper-yelled from a table that we passed. He looked back, startled, but smiled when he realized who it was.

"Hey, Izzy."

Izzy looked stunning today. Like stop-you-in-your-tracks stunning. Her long black twists rested on one shoulder, and her golden-brown skin seemed to glow against the white of her oversized button-up. Dark jeans and crisp white sneakers peeked out from beneath the table, elevating the whole look. She was mesmerizing.

"What are you guys doing here?" she said. Her eyes settled on Devlin, and she frowned in confusion, before turning back to Ellis and quirking a brow.

"We're, um, researching something?" Ellis hesitated, unsure of how to explain this weird group of strangers spending a Thursday morning at the library.

"Research? Wait," she said, her eyes narrowing at Ellis. She took a second to look at the rest of us, her eyes settling on Devlin. "Are you staying at Wildwood Motel too?"

Devlin nodded.

"Ellis, don't tell me this is about Room 9 again."

He nodded. Clearly, she was well aware of Ellis's research, or at least his concerns. She paused, giving him a long look.

"Can I help? If I have to read one more scholarly article about the repercussions of reading cultural identity as a static being versus a dynamic becoming, I'm going to cry."

He looked around, trying to gauge our reactions, but I shrugged. I liked her company, but it was his call to make. We were the ones following him deeper down the rabbit hole.

"Sure," he said.

"Great."

She shoved her books into her backpack, shut her laptop, and followed us. Judging by the stares she was getting for all the noise she was making, the people a table over seemed glad to be rid of her. She walked ahead and led us to a quiet, empty spot near the back. I watched as she whispered something to Ellis. He turned to look at her, eyes wide, but she just laughed at his reaction, her twists like vines dancing along her spine and shoulders. He faced forward and I snapped a quick shot of them. At the sound of the shutter, she looked back at Mira and me, studying us for a quick second, and I almost tripped over my own shoes when her eyes found mine. Mira caught my elbow to steady me, but it was too late. I could see Izzy chuckle as she looked ahead, her shoulders shaking slightly.

We spread out at the table in the end, our odd group having almost doubled in size in the span of an hour. I sat across from Ellis and Mira. Izzy was on my right and Devlin, my left. I set my things down, but as I did, my phone began vibrating on the table. My mom's face appeared on the screen. I knew she was going to have a million questions, and I didn't have the energy. I let it go to voice mail. This was a future-me problem.

"So, how did this little group form?" Izzy asked. Ellis sat with the question for a second. I could see Devlin stare at a scratch on the table. He picked at the wood, then clasped his hands together to keep from fidgeting. Ellis could tell Izzy that he came on board when we decided to forgive him for spending the day following us, then sneaking into our room while we were sleeping, but something told me she wouldn't forgive him as easily as we did. It wasn't exactly water under the bridge, but it was enough to give him a chance. Still, I wouldn't have blamed her for being suspicious.

"Mira and Layla," he said, pointing to each of us as he said our names, "are staying in Room 9."

"Oh. My condolences," she said in mock seriousness.

"I know you don't believe me, Izzy. No need to make fun of me too," he said, placing his backpack on the table with a loud thud. A librarian shelving books a few rows away shushed him.

"Sorry, sorry," Izzy said. "I'll be serious. No more jokes." She mimed zipping her mouth shut and throwing away the key.

"Why are you here if you're not going to even pretend to take this seriously?" Ellis said.

"Someone has to keep an eye on you. Plus, I needed a break from my own thesis research. Your research, though it wouldn't hold up in a peer-reviewed journal, is far more interesting." She turned her attention to Devlin. "Who's this guy?"

"Devlin. Nice to meet you," he said, smiling at her.

She didn't smile back. Her eyes were narrowed and her chin was tilted up, almost like she was looking down at him even though they were both sitting. Her arms remained crossed, like she was still trying to make up her mind about him.

"What do you do, Devlin?" She was younger than him, probably in her early twenties, but in that moment, with her sharp gaze and blunt tongue, you couldn't help but answer any question she had.

"I'm a doctor. Almost, anyway. I'm doing my residency in Chicago." And then, after a bit of silence, he continued, answering her real question, which had to be *What are you doing here*? "My wife, Madeline, stayed in that room a couple months ago. She's unwell now. She's been—hospitalized.

I had to have her admitted to a psychiatric facility. But it all started with this motel, Room 9. I came back looking for, I don't know, answers, I suppose?" he said.

She relaxed her stance a little, her shoulders unclenching at his words.

"I'm sorry to hear that."

"But you don't think it has anything to do with the room," he said, answering his own question.

"No, I don't." She looked back at Ellis. "Sorry, kid. It sucks that people died in that room, but bad luck is just unfortunate coincidence. A pattern, especially a pattern that points to a mysterious room that kills people, is not necessarily based in reality. There's always a scientific, logical explanation. You're just missing a piece of the puzzle."

I wanted to agree but kept my comments to myself. Mira knew I was skeptical, but it accomplished nothing to voice those thoughts. Best-friend duties had been invoked, and I needed to make Mira feel like she was supported, even if Izzy was making more and more sense.

"Okay. Then find it," Ellis said as he unzipped his backpack and slid one of the record books toward her.

"Find what?"

"Find the missing puzzle piece. Find the logic in the pattern. Prove me wrong."

She smiled at him, happily accepting the challenge.

"What's the plan?" I asked.

Mira took out the second book from her bag and placed it on the table.

"I'm thinking we split into groups," Ellis said. "Layla and Devlin, you two focus on research—hauntings, maybe articles about other places that show a similar pattern? I don't know. We don't have a lead here. If you have an idea, follow it, I guess."

Devlin nodded and took out his laptop. A part of me was looking forward to good old-fashioned research. We'd litter the table with stacks and stacks of tattered books, searching mythology and folklore for answers. Going decades deep until we pulled back each layer of the room's history. It almost sounded fun.

"Izzy, you take this record book. It's 1994 to 2013. Mira, you'll get 1976 to 1993. Both of you make a list of guests who stayed in Room 9. Then go down the list, trying to find any information you can on them online."

"What should we be looking for?" Mira asked.

"Anything that seems odd? If it feels like their life went off the rails? Suspicious deaths, disappearances? Honestly, I'm not sure. Trust your gut, note it, and we'll see if we have any similarities, or if it's just the eight and Madeline."

He opened his laptop. "We went digital in 2014. I can log in to our online system from here and do the same."

He looked around at all of us. "Sound good?"

"Can I point out that motel clientele isn't exactly top shelf?" Izzy said. "No offense to anyone at this table, but we're cheap, we take cash, and we don't ask many questions. Your data pool naturally leans toward the results you're already looking for."

"Then we account for that. We take our data with a grain of salt and we focus on suspicious bad luck. Not just run-of-the-mill bad luck. Good?"

She pursed her lips at him in response and reached between us to open the large book to the first page.

She rolled up her sleeves to reveal a tattoo of a fox walking up the inside of her right forearm. Its intricate lines lazily blended into one another, but its eyes were focused and alert. It was the only tattoo on her right arm. Her left was an elaborate sleeve of flowers, art, and text that created a beautiful black-lined tapestry.

She noticed me staring, not that I was being smooth.

"Sorry, they're just so pretty," I whispered.

"It's cool, I catch myself staring at them too."

"Why the fox?" I asked, looking back at her right arm. She still had room on her left arm, but it felt like it was on its own for a reason, like it was significant.

"I saw a fox once. It was pretty," she said, shrugging. "Don't let anyone tell you the only tattoos you should get are the ones that mean something. It's bullshit. We're all skin bags walking toward death."

She flipped to the first page of the records and pulled out a notebook from her backpack. I don't think I'd ever thought about getting a tattoo, but now I wanted two full-color sleeves of everything I loved and didn't love and moderately liked.

"All right," she said as she wrapped her twists around her wrist and into a high messy bun.

"How should we do this?" Devlin asked me, his voice hushed.

"You search online for any possible explanations. I'll go look for books and old town records that could help?" I suggested.

"Sounds good." He smiled, like he could tell I longed to walk down these aisles looking for any relevant books to pull. Which was fine. He could try to be friendly. Didn't mean I was going to reciprocate it. I didn't fully trust him, and a friendly smile wasn't going to change that.

I followed the signs to the back of the library and started with deeds and property titles. But soon enough I realized the motel was the first thing that was ever built in that spot. Before 1976, it was only a piece of land. There was nothing suspicious or unordinary about it, at least not anything the records would tell me. I moved on.

On the shelves, I pulled a wide array of nonfiction titles. Anything that even hinted at the paranormal, at the unexplained. Half of them felt silly, but we had no idea what we were looking for and we knew it.

I sat back down next to Devlin and laid the stack between us. He turned the books to better read the spines.

"*A History of Spirits, Seances, and Psychics*. Ah," he said, pulling one out. "*The Complete Guide to Nature's Phenomena*." He opened it and skimmed the table of contents. "Weather patterns? The lunar cycle? This is fascinating."

"Don't know what I'm looking for, but it's something. How's yours going?" I added.

"Not much progress, but focusing on folklore and paranormal sightings. Maybe whatever this is is older than time; maybe someone figured out how to stop it."

"If there's anything to stop," I mumbled mostly to myself. I was willing to dive into the research, but still, it was hard to leave all logic at the door.

He began to say something but stopped. His eyes went wide as his hands reached for his throat.

"Devlin? What's wrong?" I said. His eyes bored into mine as his face turned red. The veins in his forehead protruded as he tugged at his collar. But it was no use. He was choking, suffocating on nothing. I looked around the table hoping someone knew what to do, but we were all helpless.

Frozen. He pushed against the table and in his panic fell backward. The chair, and Devlin, clattered to the floor in a loud thud.

Suddenly, he gasped in a lungful of air. Stole mouthfuls of it like it would run out if he didn't. Mira and Ellis stood up, checking to see if he was okay. I bent down to help him up, and he took my hand as Izzy lifted his chair back into place. A librarian eyed us curiously before returning to her shelving.

"What was that?" I asked.

"I—I don't know. I just, I felt like I was suffocating, but I—I can't explain it. I don't know what happened."

He was still breathing heavy, his chest quickly rising and falling with his words.

"Do you want us to take you back to the motel? Maybe you should lie down," Mira said.

He shook his head. Filled his lungs in one big breath and slowly let it out. "I'm okay. I promise. Let's just get back to work."

"I really think—"

"No," he said, interrupting Mira. "No, let's just keep going." He flipped a page in the book in front of him, ending the conversation.

Mira and I looked at each other, at a loss for what to do next, but she just shrugged and returned to her book. If he said he was fine, he was fine. But still. It made me think of the way Mira had woken up this morning, without any control of her body. How she felt like she was drowning. I pushed the thought away and dove back into the books.

After an hour, I felt like I had barely made any progress. The world is strange and mysterious, the unexplainable commonplace. There was too much possibility, not enough facts to base anything on. Judging by Izzy's sigh, she was having the same luck.

"There's too much unknown, Ellis," Izzy said. "Even if we have the state they came from, there's multiple people who come up with that same name in that state. They could also have moved, gotten married, and changed their last name." She set her pen down, unsure of how to move forward.

"You're not wrong. We're looking for a handful of needles in a forty-seven-year-old haystack." He leaned back in his chair and stared at the ceiling. His hands gripped the edge of the table as he balanced on the back legs of his chair.

"I'm having the same problem," Mira said. "I'm not getting anywhere. I've found three deaths, but none are suspicious, and we're looking at records from the seventies. Obviously some people are going to be dead. More so in mine than yours," she said to Izzy, nodding toward her book.

"Of course," Ellis said, his chair landing forward with a loud thud. "Because you're looking at the seventies." His eyes lit up, like he was onto something and he couldn't tell us fast enough. "Eight deaths in forty years. But they happen more and more frequently. The years between the deaths goes from twelve years to nine to seven, six, five, three, and two. Which means, if there was anything that happened to guests who didn't die, it would have to follow the same pattern. They'd happen with more frequency in the later years. So, there would barely be anything to find in the first book. Hell, it would take half the second book to start noticing anything suspicious." He realized he was getting louder and leaned forward, trying his best to whisper.

"Forget the first book. We need to focus on the online records system and the second half of this," he said, pointing to the newer record book. "Start backward. Anything worth noting would have happened more recently."

It made sense, I guess. In this odd, nothing-made-sense sort of way.

"All right, Elly. I like your thinking. I'll keep my comments to myself for now," Izzy said.

"Thank you."

"We'll share this one and check off each name as we go?" Izzy said to Mira. She nodded, and they dove back in. Devlin and I looked at the stack of books between us, at the scribbled notes and question marks I'd made on the page. There was nothing to do but keep going. One way or another, we were going to get an answer. I just hoped they were prepared for a disappointing one.

TWENTY-SEVEN

Mira

People had come and gone, and judging by the waning light, we were hours deep into this. Long enough to get hungry again and have Izzy grab a box of doughnuts that we kept hidden in a backpack on the table. But the things I had learned in the past few hours, the things I'd learned about these strangers, I didn't think I would ever be able to forget them. It felt like I was vibrating with energy, and I wasn't sure how to contain it all.

"Guys, listen to this," I said, reading the article. "'Two pedestrians were injured when a vehicle drove through the Madison, Wisconsin, post office, according to the Madison Police Department. Officers responded to a 911 call where a man was reported to have abruptly veered away from traffic and into the south-side wall of the building. The driver, confirmed to be Nathan Stranton, forty-two, was not harmed in the incident but resisted arrest when cops arrived on the scene. What happens next was caught on camera. A warning that the video below is graphic.'"

I pulled out my headphones from the jack so they could all listen and clicked on the video that a bystander a few feet away had shot of the arrest. Aside from a nosebleed, Nathan looked fine. A cop attempted to handcuff him, but Nathan pushed against him, trying to get his hands free. He shouted, "I can't live like this. Let me die."

After slamming his head back into the cop's nose, Nathan, with his hands cuffed behind him, ran into open traffic. No less than a second later, he was hit by a truck that sent him flying into the air. He was facedown on the pavement, one leg bent beneath him when he landed. His hands were still wound behind him. He was dead by the time the ambulance came.

"My God. That was the worst one yet," Devlin said. As we all sat there processing what we had seen, Layla slowly pulled out a doughnut. She noticed us all staring and quickly chewed her mouthful.

"I think I eat when I'm nervous," she said quietly.

I scrolled to the bottom of the article to find a photo of Nathan Stranton taken the year prior, according to the credit beneath it. Around parts of him was a hazy light, like the focus was off. Or like someone had quickly tried to edit away unnatural warping. It reminded me of Layla's photos. Or the way I looked in them, encompassed by something that was not there. Maybe I was searching. But this wasn't

the only time I'd seen something like this today when looking through articles. Paranoia could only go so far until it
found some logic to land on.

"What year did he stay and when did that happen?" Ellis
asked. I knew he was trying to stay focused, impartial, but I
could tell that that one hit him harder than the others. We
hadn't seen video of anything today, and this was jarring.
Maybe for Ellis more than anyone. He'd had a story in his
head for so long. Had thought he knew the full magnitude
of this room. And now to have it violently ripped away at the
sight of this? It was a hard thing to accept. He swallowed and
picked up his pen.

"2009 and 2011."

Ellis made a note of it on the Excel sheet he was using
to keep track of it all. Nathan was only the tip of the iceberg. We'd been logging our findings for hours, reading
suspicious or noteworthy news articles and obituaries out
loud. We had dozens of entries.

A few minutes later, Izzy spoke up. "'Police responded
to a disturbance call in Toledo, Ohio, to find Luca Gherton, twenty-eight, and Stacey Wimbrol, twenty-seven, dead
from gunshot wounds in an apparent murder suicide. Police
believe Wimbrol shot Gherton, then killed herself.'"

On and on it went. A long list of names that only kept
growing at the same pace as the frequency of Room 9 deaths.

I knew logically there were tons of factors to consider. Guests from the seventies, even if they died or something happened to them soon after, wouldn't come up in a Google search as easily as something in the last ten years. I knew that people died, because everyone died, knew that there were things about this room no amount of research would ever let us in on. But this had to be something. Almost a third of the people had something worth noting. An unnatural death, a murder, a suicide, a psych ward. Did we need more proof that the room made people feel things, see things? No matter how it all happened, something about Room 9 was real and not imagined.

I thrilled in the knowledge that I wasn't insane or sick or needing to admit myself to the nearest psych ward. But the joy was short-lived when I realized what this meant. I'd fallen into a trap I had no way of escaping. Others had left the room, and here they were, entries in an Excel sheet.

"How about you guys?" I said, turning to Layla and Devlin.

"Yes? And no? Nothing conclusive. Haunted hotels aren't that strange. Most of them are tourist attractions. But almost all have to do with ghosts, and Mira, you didn't mention any ghost sightings."

I shook my head.

"Not ghosts that were guests, anyway," he clarified.

"Fun fact," Layla said into the silence. "In 2007, the police force in Brighton, UK, spent a summer deploying more officers during full moons because they were convinced it was the cause of violent crime. Granted, I checked the guest stays against a lunar calendar, and there's no correlation, so ..." She trailed off.

"I've looked at midwestern folklore, mythology, hauntings, religion," Devlin said. "It could be any of these or none of them."

"My money's on just plain cursed," Layla said as she stacked the books and put away her notes.

We all sat with that for a minute, with the knowledge of what we'd learned about the past guests and our inability to do anything about it. My heart sped up at the inescapable nature of it all.

"I'm going to put those books back." I stood up and grabbed them before anyone could stop me.

"I can go with you. I'll show you where they were," Layla said, already half out of her seat.

"It's okay. I saw what aisle you went into." I smiled to soften my words. She sat back down and nodded. I just needed a moment alone. A second to gather my thoughts before I could join them and figure out next steps. My chest was getting tighter with every second I sat here. I walked down an aisle of books, looking for where Layla pulled these from, when I heard it. The sound of waves crashing to shore.

"No, no, no," I whispered to myself.

The scent of sunscreen came next. I closed my eyes, balled my hands into fists, but I could feel grains of sand beneath my fingernails then. In the back of my throat was the taste of salt water, like I had swallowed wrong or done a flip underwater without holding my nose. I was too terrified to open my eyes. Too scared to find myself on that beach from a summer ago. But what I saw was so much worse.

A few shelves away stood Khalil.

He was in his swim shorts, water dripping from their blue hems. The wet gray tint to his skin shone under the library lights. He looked at me, his eyes wide and pleading, but said nothing. We stood there in still silence, staring at each other. When he finally opened his mouth to speak, only salt water came out. I reached toward him, but before my fingers could touch skin, he faded away in a wisp of gray-and-blue smoke, no trace of him but the memory forever imprinted on my mind. I tried to breathe, but it was impossible. My throat was constricting with each lungful of air. My lungs felt small, fragile. I slid down to the floor and put my head between my knees, trying to take short, shallow breaths until the panic subsided. Eventually, I stood up, squared my shoulders, and went back.

"Okay, I think it's time to call it," Ellis said as I walked up to the group. He closed his laptop and stared at the open record book on the table.

"Food. I need food," Layla said, snapping him out of it.

"Do you guys want to grab pizza? I'm craving Roberta's, and I still have some time before my shift." Izzy checked her phone as she said it. "An hour, to be exact. Damn, it's almost seven. Let's move, people. Pizza waits for no woman."

We packed up our things and left. I knew I should tell them what I'd seen, but what was the point? If we'd learned anything today, it was that this was bigger than any of us. It was that I was more alone here than any of them could understand. It was getting dark by the time we stepped outside, the sky a dark orange and purple with pink-tinged clouds. The buildings were golden where the last of the sun's rays landed.

"Where did you park?" Ellis asked as he shifted his bag from one shoulder to the other, already eager to set it down.

"Behind the library," Izzy said. "We can drop off our bags and walk to the pizza place. The weather is too nice."

"Oh, okay," Ellis said. He grumbled something under his breath and led the way. Izzy had us put all our bags in her trunk. She didn't bother locking her car before walking away and I knew Layla was glad to have kept her camera on her, the strap worn across her body. The pizza place was a block down and around the corner. When Devlin offered to pay, no one stopped him. I think he still felt bad sneaking into our room last night, so I didn't feel bad letting him.

From the window, I could see it was a small shop, a counter and standing room only. The words *Roberta's Pizzeria* were painted in red across the white wall behind the counter. Devlin went in to place our order, and the rest of us stayed outside. I reveled in the scent that wafted out when he opened the door to go inside, letting the warm smell of marinara and dough fill my nostrils where the salt water and sunscreen were only a few minutes ago.

My eyes refocused on the window glass to find my reflection staring back. Around me though was that same strange warping from Layla's photos, except here, it was moving. Faint but intelligible as it wound its way around me. One end of it disappeared where it met the door, but the other end trailed behind me, weaving around Layla and Izzy, almost avoiding them, until it settled near Ellis's feet. It was a breathing thing, moving and shifting around me, even when I took a step to either side. I touched my shoulder, almost expecting to feel the weight of it in my hand, but of course, there was nothing there.

"Layla, do you see that?" I asked. She looked over to where I was staring but only seemed confused.

"Devlin?" she said, looking through the glass and inside the pizza place.

"Never mind." I held down a sigh and joined the others. What use was it? I was alone. I resisted the urge to look over my shoulder and check for the bending light, the warping haze. I didn't need to see it. I knew it still shrouded me no matter where I stood.

"So," Ellis started. "After a long day of research, data, and analysis, what are your thoughts now?"

Layla and Izzy looked at each other for a few seconds, trying to make up their minds. I knew Layla was trying her best to go along with this, to support me because she knew I needed her to, not because she was convinced. But maybe, after today, she wouldn't need to pretend.

"Fine. Maybe, just maybe, you guys are onto something," Izzy finally said. Layla didn't protest, and I took that as a bittersweet win. I didn't want to be right. But if I had to be, I was glad she was on my side through it.

"I still don't understand why some people were fine and others aren't. I don't feel anything in that room. Except worry for you, Mira," Layla added. "We all heard those stories, the news reports, that video. All of it, one way or another, linked back to that room. Clearly, something is happening to you when we're in it. What's going to happen when we leave?"

I wanted more than anything to reassure her and say everything was going to be fine. That this room wasn't going to kill me. That we'd finish our trip, our senior year, and years from now talk about that one time where, for a few days, we thought our motel room was watching us.

But I didn't know any of that, not when the memory of Khalil at the library was still seared into my brain, or the slithering distortions in the glass. All I knew was that something I couldn't explain was happening to me and knowing that it probably happened to countless other people did not feel reassuring. It only scared me.

I couldn't tell her that I saw Khalil everywhere, that when he wasn't a crystal-clear image turned to smoke, he was in the waiter's hands, the bend of someone's shoulders, that I didn't know what was the room and what was me anymore.

So instead, I lied. "Don't worry about me. I'm going to be fine. We're going to figure this out. I know we will."

She reached out and squeezed my hand for a second, and the feel of it rooted me back to her. I didn't know if she could see through my bullshit, but holding her hand, I almost convinced myself that everything really was going to be okay.

Almost.

TWENTY-EIGHT

There are many ways to delve deeper into the secrets people hide. Dreams are the easiest. A mirror into the psyche: With the right prodding, well-shaped dreams keep no secrets. A vulnerable sleeper has no say when every dark thought and delicious emotion comes spilling out.

Thoughts are harder, better protected, but not invincible. They need effort, power. The buried ones need time. With precision, it is not impossible to slither into them if one looks for the right cracks, the open seams. Then it is only a matter of bringing darker thoughts closer to the light.

Things though, things are discarded treats turned treasures. Objects are remnants of people's pasts, memories etched onto their surfaces. Like Mira's leather jacket and the fear she felt sitting near the pool two nights ago. It was intrinsically linked to the remorse she felt when her father gifted it to her seven months prior for her seventeenth birthday. Her green T-shirt thrown on top of her suitcase and the anxiety she felt yesterday morning were marred with the taste of hope from last night.

These things, splayed out across the room, are an education on Mira Hamdi.

TWENTY-NINE

Layla

I pulled my hand away from Mira's. Sometimes, it seemed like it was all I ever did. Whenever she was too close, whenever my heart stuttered because of a fleeting touch or warm smile, it was all I could think to do. But Izzy was staring at me now with this all-knowing look, like she could read my mind. Whatever. She could make up her own ideas, but she didn't know anything about any of this. It was easier not to look at Izzy if I was annoyed. I didn't like how much I liked looking at her. Sure, my heart beat for Mira like she was the blood pumping through it, but looking at Izzy was like looking at a painting: All you wanted to do was stand there and take it in.

Devlin came out of Roberta's with two pizzas in hand. He had his phone pressed between his ear and shoulder.

"Want to head back and eat this by the pool?" Izzy asked us as she took the two boxes from him. He mouthed "Thank you" to her and kept listening to whatever was happening on the other end of his call.

"Sounds good," Ellis said. After that we somehow shifted into groups. Mira and Ellis fell back a few yards behind us, and Devlin trailed behind them as we all made our way back to Izzy's car.

I wondered how Mira was really feeling with our recent wealth of knowledge, if she believed what she'd said earlier about making it out of here in one piece. I doubted she was as okay as she said. Sure, it was kind of her to not want to worry me, but I knew better. That place was forever tainted with death, and what we'd learned today proved it was so much worse than any of us thought. Mira and I would leave tomorrow, but I couldn't understand how Ellis and Izzy could bear to stay. How Ellis's mom could walk past that room every day after finding her husband's dead body in it. After doing what she did when she found it. If I were her, I would sell the place, take Ellis, and move as far away as I could.

"You look very deep in thought," Izzy said.

I wanted to brush it off, but I knew I'd only keep thinking about it. "Ellis told us about what his mom did when—when she found Ellis's dad. I don't know, I just keep thinking about how that would affect someone. How do you just move on from that?"

If Izzy was surprised by the topic, she didn't show it. She was quiet for a moment, contemplating how to answer.

"Elena went through a pretty dark period after Noah's death. She didn't come down much, didn't answer calls, didn't really say more than a few words at a time. It was like she was stuck in a loop. You could see it on her face, the way she kept playing it all back, looking for what she'd missed, trying to explain to herself why she did what she did those three days. And then one day, she came downstairs, sat in the back room, and went through the books. Something Noah had always done. No one else was there to do it. Ellis tried once, but the kid barely passed algebra." She laughed at the thought and continued.

"When I asked her what had changed, she said, *I have to start forgiving myself. No one else will.* She still has a long way to go, but she's trying. I think in grief, we do things even we don't understand. Our bodies just process trauma differently."

I nodded, unsure of what to say to that. It made sense. It was just unfortunate that it did.

She smiled reassuringly. "You don't have to look so sad. She's okay, I promise."

We walked in silence for a while. For once, the quiet was comfortable.

I pulled my phone out of my pocket when it vibrated with a text. The group chat I had with my sisters kept pinging.

MOUNA: Checking to see if you're alive. Mom is convinced that you've been murdered.

MOUNA: I don't really feel like planning your funeral right now, so call her back.

DINA: If you have been murdered, dibs on your car.

MOUNA: No way, Dina. Wait your turn. That car is mine. You can have it if I've been murdered.

DINA: Stop giving me motive.

I texted back, **Not dead but I appreciate the concern. I'll call her tonight. Busy right now,** and put the phone away. Being the oldest was mostly exhausting, but as much as I hated sharing a room with two little sisters, it'd been a week since I'd seen their faces. When I was home, all I ever wanted was a moment alone, but now the idea of being stuck in a room with them didn't seem so bad. Dina was only twelve, but she had gotten into the habit of trying on my makeup the second I left the room, the same makeup I was hiding from my mom. It wouldn't have been so frustrating if she didn't deny it with peach blush on her cheeks and shaky eyeliner on her lids.

Mouna didn't care much for makeup or stealing my clothes or touching my stuff, except my books, which I never minded. She'd just turned fifteen and liked oversized hoodies and being pissed off at our parents. She shaved her head over Christmas break, and neither of my parents appreciated the surprise. For the next week, my mom cried every time she looked at her. Most days, I felt like the mediator between them, but still, we were close. All three of us were. It was surprising to know that a week away left me missing them. I could only imagine what moving away for college would be like. It was weird to think that I'd only see them every few months.

If I left at all, that is. My parents weren't paying for my college anyway. I would figure it out myself. I was already shooting senior photos. I could start doing weddings and engagement sessions to pay for school. Loans would be available to me. I didn't need to choose Parsons because of the scholarship. I just wanted to be in my dream program, enjoying college and the city with Mira by my side. I'd work harder and it would be worth it. I could find a way to make Chicago happen. But it was never about that, and I knew it. Arab kids, especially Arab girls, didn't leave home for college. They just didn't. I knew my parents expected me to go to a college that was a drivable distance away. Somewhere safe, where they could keep an eye on me. Where I could have a curfew and feel like it was a four-year extension of high school. Just more difficult. It was exhausting to think about. Nearly as exhausting as thinking about how they would react if I told them I wanted to go elsewhere.

It seemed silly to worry about any of this after the two days we'd had. What was it, really, in the grand scheme of things? I had a mystery room to think about and a Mira to worry about. It was plenty.

I put my phone away and opened one of the pizza boxes she was holding, just a smidge, to steal a loose black olive near the edge. Izzy moved the pizzas to rest on one arm, opened the box all the way, and pulled out an entire slice, the cheese oozing all the way down.

"I feel like I haven't eaten in years," Izzy said. "Take one; I can't be the only one drooling at the smell wafting out of this box."

I grabbed one that looked like it had a few more olives than the others and bit into it. Then of course did that thing where you breathe in and out quickly because the cheese feels like lava in your mouth.

"So, I noticed you were making eyes at Mira today."

I choked on my mouthful of pizza and Izzy laughed.

"Not sure what you're talking about," I said, though I'm pretty sure choking on my pizza gave me away.

"Oh, come on. I'm not even talking about how you guys

held hands for like a full five seconds back there while staring deeply into each other's eyes, which, granted, should be enough proof. No, I'm talking about all the glances you snuck back at the library. Or when she left to use the bathroom and you watched her walk away. Or how you kept looking around the whole time, waiting for her to come back."

"I just— I wanted to make sure she didn't get lost on the way back. We've never been here before." I didn't even sound believable to me.

Izzy stared at me, one eyebrow raised, like *Who do you think you're lying to right now?*

I started to defend myself, but what was the point? Izzy saw right through me, and after tomorrow, she'd be a stranger again. I looked back and saw that Mira and Ellis were in the middle of their own conversation, too distracted and far away to hear ours. I toyed with the words, felt their shape on my tongue, and decided to hell with it.

"I love her," I said, and the world didn't end.

"And Mira has no idea?"

"I think she suspects. I'm sure a part of her knows. But I haven't come out, not that I even know what I'd be coming out as."

"That makes sense. Sometimes, it takes a little while longer to figure shit out."

"Sure, but it's more complicated than that. My family

is—" I hesitated here, trying to find the right words. My parents weren't conservative. If anything, they were progressive. They were self-proclaimed feminists. They attended protests. They believed in free health care and gun reform. But voting for Obama twice wasn't a get-out-of-jail-free card. They were kind and accepting and loved me and my sisters. But their love had limits. "My family is Muslim. It occasionally comes with its own set of shitty opinions. Being Arab has its pros and cons. Sure, the food is great. The homophobia? Not so much."

"Shitty parents sound like a big con."

"They're not bad people," I said. I wasn't sure why I was defending them. "Mira's family and mine are two of the only Muslim families where we live. They're not even that close, and I think not having a community makes my parents hold on even tighter to ideas they brought with them. It's the only perspective they've known. You spend your whole life being told something is wrong, filling it with shame and secrecy. Most everyone back in Egypt validates the very thing they're telling you by shunning anyone who identifies as anything LGBTQIA adjacent. It's like a self-fulfilling prophecy of hate. It would take a lot to fight against that."

"Maybe you coming out to them could be that."

I wanted to believe her, but I knew better. I thought about a talk my sisters and I had with my dad a few months ago. Some discussion that somehow wound its way to gay rights. And when Mouna asked him, *How would you react if one of us was gay*, I wondered if she suspected when she asked or if she was just curious about our dad's answer herself. I didn't know if I had imagined the quick glance she had thrown in my direction. He had very clearly said, *It would change my relationship with that person.* That it was unnatural and he couldn't find it in himself to ever support something like that. He was honest, and I'm sure there was something admirable to be said about that, but the truth was staring me in the face, and it was better I accept it and move on than try to fight it.

"It'd have to be something bigger than me," I told Izzy. "I'm not enough." A quiet part of me wondered if this was all one lengthy excuse, if I was finding a bit of comfort in being able to shut the door on this future by focusing on the fact that my parents would never approve of us. Was I using my parents to avoid confronting the root of all of this? That I was too scared to tell Mira how I felt because what we already had was too important to risk. She was too important.

We walked in silence for a bit, and I could tell she wanted to say more, but there really wasn't more to say.

"Mira likes you too. In case you were wondering. In case that changes anything."

Except that. She could say that.

"You can't possibly know that. We just met you."

"Call it feminine intuition. Call it gaydar. Hell, call it common sense. That girl is just waiting for you to come out to her, hoping you feel the same way she does."

I looked back at Mira, trying to see if there was any truth to this or if Izzy was just talking out of her ass. I raised the camera and clicked. Framing Mira on the left with Ellis next to her and Devlin, farther back, on the right. Mira looked at me as she listened to something Ellis was saying. The warping was still there, tugging at her edges. Now, after everything we'd learned, all I felt was dread at the sight of it. A breeze moved through her warm honey curls, lifting a section across her face before it drifted past her.

It made me think of the first time I was surprised by my own feelings toward Mira. We were in the library, studying for midterms. Algebra or geometry, I couldn't remember now. Mira sat across from me in this glass room that overlooked the children's books. She had these oversized headphones on, but even those couldn't subdue her curls from forming a caramel halo around her head. She wore a hoodie that we had bleached together a few weeks before—mine a mess, hers purposeful and cool—and looked utterly calm as she worked out the equations in her notebook.

I, on the other hand, remember feeling so frustrated

that I couldn't figure out where I was going wrong with the math problem. I was staring at the paper, this close to scribbling out all the work I'd done, when I threw the pencil down and stared at it, willing it to make sense. It didn't. Mira reached forward, ever so slowly, and gently wound a loose strand of my hair around her index finger. I looked at her as she did it, my eyes trained on hers, but she was focused on my hair and the way it softly looped around her finger.

Then, just as gently, she tucked it back into the messy bun it had escaped from. As she pulled her hand away, her thumb grazed my cheek and I just about stopped breathing. She smiled at me like nothing had happened and went back to her own math problems. It was as simple and as complicated as that.

"You don't know what you're talking about," I said.

But Mira's smile had been soft and her eyes warm, and more than anything, I wanted to believe what Izzy saw.

THIRTY

Mira

I couldn't stop thinking about everything we'd learned, about the overwhelming magnitude of it all and how trapped I felt by it. Thoughts and images of Khalil seemed to permeate every conversation, every thought. And now, as we walked back in silence to the motel, I couldn't escape the image of Khalil drowning again and again. I could almost hear the ocean. Even in the middle of Indiana, there it was, strong and persistent, an underlying current beneath it all.

"You okay?" Ellis asked.

We had fallen into step next to each other. Layla and Izzy were ahead of us, not so smoothly sneaking a slice of pizza from the boxes Izzy was holding. The sun lit them both just right and I quickly snapped a picture of them. Devlin was a few feet behind us, still on the phone. He seemed to be talking to his wife's hospital, trying to check in on her. He had his phone tucked between his ear and his shoulder while his hands tried to light a cigarette in the breeze. Strange to see a doctor, of all people, smoke. But who was I to judge an unhealthy coping mechanism? Maybe it was a bad habit he picked up after Madeline was committed.

Ellis looked at me, clearly concerned, and as much as I wanted to brush it off, smile, and change the subject, I couldn't. I felt drained and exhausted and alone. I'd spent so long avoiding the details of Khalil's death. I wasn't sure if I could do it anymore. I had never felt like I could share them with my parents, with Layla. I was too afraid that they would never look at me the same way again. That once I told them the truth, it would be all they'd ever see. I didn't feel like making myself into a stranger to the people I cared about most.

But Ellis.

If anyone could understand, it would be Ellis, who knew death so intimately. And at this point, keeping it to myself only felt like I was swallowing a grenade and waiting for the inevitable.

"You know how I told you about my brother?"

"I remember," he said, seeing my hesitation. "You don't have to tell me anything. I didn't mean to make you talk about it if you didn't want to."

"No, I—I need to. I didn't tell you how it happened. I didn't tell anyone. So let me say it, okay?"

He nodded.

The people in my life, Layla included, knew the story up to this point. Knew that the story ended with a dead brother. But I always skipped over what came before, always swallowed it down, deeper every time I had to tell it.

"I had swum out, but my feet were firmly on the ground, water just at my shoulders. I called him over, Khalil, told him to swim in deeper. He was only a little shorter than me, so it seemed like a safe depth. He was by himself, the water at his waist, and I knew why; I knew that he hated the water, hated putting his head beneath the surface, that he had only made it that far because my parents were being annoying about coming all the way to the beach just for him to sit in the sand with a book for three hours. I knew I should have let him be. He was fine alone. He always seemed to prefer it. But I kept calling, pushing him, trying to pull him in deeper. I remember saying, *Come closer, don't be a baby*. I knew I was being mean. But I told myself he needed some tough love."

I wanted to end the story there. Wanted to let Khalil tell me no, spend a few more minutes in waist-deep waters, and make it back to his towel and the rest of his book and my parents.

"So, he started walking forward, still refusing to go beneath the surface. I remember his hair was still dry by the time he reached me." I smiled at the memory, and Ellis smiled too, hesitantly.

"Somehow, I convinced him to float on his back with me. But the tide was stronger than we thought, and after a few seconds it carried us farther than either of us thought it would. Suddenly, our feet couldn't touch the ground anymore, and the sand felt impossibly far away." I paused, collecting myself, and again, Ellis didn't interrupt, just let me say what I needed to say. Let me get it all out.

I told Ellis how the sea dipped. It wasn't this consistent decline that got deeper and deeper. There were sinkholes and shifts and trenches and God knows what else. The seafloor was its own beast, its topography dark and as temperamental as the water's surface.

He listened as I told him how my brother tried to stand up, realized he couldn't touch the ground, and the fear took over. I'd never liked being that deep in myself, but it would have been fine. I would have ducked my head under and started swimming toward shore until I could feel the ground beneath my feet again, but it was different with Khalil.

He panicked.

Instantly.

And survival kicked in. He grabbed on to the nearest thing he could, me, and tried to stay above the surface. But it brought us both under.

I paused, just for a second, and pushed through as quickly as I could. I told him how I could hear Khalil's muffled screams of *Help* from beneath the surface. He'd had his chin just above the water, staying up by pressing into my shoulders, ten half-moon scars still visible today in the light. First, he screamed for help in English, then, realizing no one could understand him there, in Arabic. He didn't speak much Arabic. Enough to understand when our extended family needed something from him but not enough to reply as fluently as they would have liked. But in seconds he was screaming for help in Arabic, hoping his voice was loud enough for someone to hear.

"I don't think he fully knew I was there. I think he felt alone in that moment."

I told Ellis how I couldn't breathe. In trying to get to the surface, I'd pulled Khalil down, used his weight to keep me above the surface. I wasn't thinking. Neither of us was. I knew that. I knew that all either of us wanted was to get above the water. For air to fill our lungs. But I pushed him under and I kept him there. For a few seconds too long, all I could think about was air and help and not dying, and somewhere in the midst of all of that, I sacrificed my brother for it.

"By the time someone saw us, it was too late. Two guys swam over and pulled us to shore. My brother wasn't breathing."

"Mira," he said. His eyes were wide as he stared at me, shock written all over his stricken face. It didn't look like he believed it when he said, "It's not yo—"

"Don't. It is. If I hadn't pressured him into coming closer. If I had left him alone. If I had been a big sister and let him live. If I had done a million things but what I did, he would be here. I'm responsible for that, and I'm the one who's going to live with that."

I could see him resisting the urge to say *I'm sorry*. He faced forward and kept walking. It was surprisingly easier to tell this stranger about the deepest, darkest part of me than to share it with Layla. It didn't feel better to share it—that wasn't it. But I didn't feel worse for telling him. Maybe only for bringing it all back to the surface for the first time since it happened. Like I was getting a taste of what it would feel like not to have to hide this all the time.

Like maybe I was beginning to face what I had done.

"My mom took down all the photos of my dad. Sometimes it feels like he's never existed. And right after those moments where I've forgotten about him, I can't help but hate myself for it. Not because I've forgotten about him. Because a part of me enjoyed the peace I felt when I did." He paused for a moment, then continued. "I blame myself for a lot too," he said.

Layla looked back at us then, as if in response to what

Ellis had said, but I didn't think they could hear us. I definitely couldn't hear what they were talking about. She lifted the camera to her eye and clicked. I glanced at the lens and turned my attention to Ellis.

"I never had a great relationship with my dad, and I'll always wonder if I'd had a better relationship with him, if we talked, if I knew what he was feeling, maybe things would've been different. Maybe the room wouldn't have had an effect on him, maybe he would have been stronger than it. I don't know." He looked like there was more he wanted to say, like there was something else that was eating him up, but he hesitated for a second, looked at me, and focused on a small rock ahead of him that he kicked a few feet away.

"I think you're asking questions you don't want answered."

He nodded, agreeing, and we kept walking, the motel now in sight.

THIRTY-ONE

Sometimes, it is lonely inside this room. Hours, days, weeks go by before someone enters, before they scatter their things across this floor and begin to dream of moments they would rather forget. Mira is welcome reprieve.

Now the edges of her are near, only feet away from the door. Her familiar scent wades in.

But she is not alone.

Mira walks past, surrounded by a group of people, some more captivating than others. Ellis, little Elly, they call him, comes closer and closer still. There is so much lurking beneath his skin, aching to leak out. Soon, it will all spill over. Like father, like son.

Devlin, the man behind last night's brief interruption, is just as enthralling. Oh, how brief his visit was, how delicious it tasted. For a few seconds, their pain and worry and shame and secrets waft into the room. It is barely a taste. The aroma that lingers around them is irresistible. Together, they move as a pack, and slowly, the three feel it roll over them. An overwhelming sense of dread.

They disappear around the corner, all out of reach. For now, the room waits, listening. It has waited for years. It has learned patience, an easy task when some things are inevitable.

THIRTY-TWO

Layla

We rounded the corner and saw the pool, its blue light filling the entire space. The sun was setting now, the sky dimming with every minute. We took the back corner of the deck and spread out. I saw Mira choose the farthest seat from the pool, avoiding looking at the water. I wanted to take her far from here, but the most I could do was offer a small distraction.

"No one move. I need a picture. This whole trip has been too weird not to have something to remember you all by," I said. I placed the camera on an empty chair, raised the ISO, lowered the shutter speed to make up for the dimming sky, and set the timer. I squeezed in next to Mira, and Devlin sat on her other side. Izzy sat to my left and Ellis squeezed in between us, choosing the ground over the edge of a seat. Mira's hand rested an inch from mine on the plastic chair, and I ached to hold it. To stretch one pinkie toward hers and see if she would intertwine her hand with mine. What did one do with all this damn yearning? By the time I heard the shutter, I realized I was so distracted by the smell of her lavender-and-lilac shampoo that I forgot to smile.

I grabbed my camera and checked the photo. What an odd group we made. I don't know why the memory of the first day of junior year flashed through my mind right then. It was Khalil's first day of high school, and Mira was feeling protective. I remember him standing at the edge of the cafeteria and looking around for a familiar face. He held a tray of pizza, tater tots, and chocolate milk. The kid looked so lost, an unmoving stone in a sea of oblivious students. Mira stood up and waved him over, and though he hadn't asked if he could sit with us on the first day, the relief on his face was palpable.

He made some friends soon after that, but I remembered those first few days fondly, the way Mira took over in her usual Mira way until he found his footing. I'm sure she was happy for him to have found his people, but I could tell she was also a little sad he didn't need us anymore.

I took off my sneakers and sat down at the edge of the pool, letting my feet dip into the cool water. The hem of my dress floated on the surface, the water slowly making its way up the fabric. Devlin joined me on the other side of the corner, sitting cross-legged near the pool stairs so that he wouldn't get his jeans wet. Ellis stretched out in one

chair, while Mira and Izzy took the one across from him. Izzy balanced the pepperoni pizza box on a small, wobbly table between them and handed Devlin and me the other box with the veggie pizza, since I didn't eat pork and Devlin was vegetarian. He paused for a second when he saw the two missing slices but grabbed one anyway.

Mira took a bite of her slice and leaned back in the chair. I looked at her, thinking about what Izzy had said. Maybe she was onto something. Maybe it was possible that Mira saw me that way. But what did it matter when I was so adamant about keeping things the way they were?

People were dying and I was wasting time fantasizing about something I'd decided could never happen.

"So, what have we learned?" I asked, forcing my attention away from places it wanted to visit.

"A lot, actually," Ellis said as he set down his half-eaten slice and wiped the grease from his hands on his shirt. He took out the large record book from his bag to reach his laptop and opened the Excel grid he had been updating all day. He scrolled through it with one hand and picked up his slice with the other.

"If we look at this chronologically, based on when they first stayed in the room, I don't know how anyone can deny that something is happening. If they survive the room, then the time between stay and notable incident gets shorter and shorter every year."

"So, what does that mean?" Mira asked.

"It's not like more people are staying in that room now than ten years ago. That number holds pretty steady. So, it has to mean—"

"That whatever that room is, it's getting stronger," Izzy finished for him. "My God, I feel ridiculous saying that out loud," she muttered.

Ellis nodded, confirming that was his own conclusion too. "And that what happens to people is based on the people themselves."

"How?" Devlin said. His eyebrows were furrowed, and he was clearly annoyed by the claim.

"No, he's right," Izzy jumped in. "Think about it. It's the only factor we can't account for. If when they stayed or how long they stayed, whether they were alone or with someone—or any other factor we've been able to note—doesn't show a pattern, then the only uncontrolled variable is the person inside Room 9 and whatever trauma or experiences or mental state or history they brought inside with them. If the room wants them, it has to be the determining factor in whether they can be strong enough to beat the room."

"I resent that statement," Devlin said. "My wife isn't in a psych ward because she's weak. It's like cancer. This whole mentality of beating it because you're stronger than it, it's bullshit. People don't die from cancer because they weren't strong enough. Sometimes the thing is beyond you. There's only so much that's within our power, and that room is a cancer."

We were all quiet for moment. No one knew what to say. I quietly grabbed another slice.

"You're right. I'm sorry. I shouldn't have said that," Izzy said. "I just meant we all have baggage, things that make up our whole, and it's a possibility that the room feeds on that in some way, that our histories affect our future after that room."

"Makes sense," I said. "Also explains why I can't see or hear what Mira sees and hears."

There was quiet for a moment, then Mira asked, "Can I see that photo of all of us?"

"Right now?"

"Really quick. I just want to check something."

Everyone watched as I turned on the camera and flipped to the last picture.

"Here," I said, handing it to her.

She zoomed in and scanned the photo, looking for something.

"What about death?" Mira offered into the silence.

"What do you mean?" Izzy asked next to her. She leaned in close to look at the photo. Mira looked around for a second, hesitant to offer up her idea, but kept going.

"Since we've gotten here, there's been something weird all around me, something warped, in all the photos I'm in.

The longer I'm here, the closer it gets. Stronger. Tighter."
She swallowed and kept going. "Devlin, pictures of you have
a similar effect. Ellis, yours do too but it's not as strong,
like it can't hold on to you as well. Which could be because
you haven't been inside the room. It knows us. You, it only
knows of."

They both stood up to get a closer look at the photo.
She was right. Even though Izzy and I were between them,
the warping still found its way to the others. It twisted
everything it touched, distorting everything in its slithering
path. They sat back down, unsure what to make of it.

"It's probably just your camera," Devlin said.

"Do you really believe that?" she asked. The look on his
face said it all. She continued.

"I saw it today. In my reflection at the pizza shop.
Fainter than the photos, but it was there. All around me."

"Is that what you were asking me?" I asked quietly.
I felt my eyebrows knitting together, apologetic for what I
couldn't see.

She nodded.

"Why didn't you say something? Why did you keep it
to yourself?"

She shrugged. "I saw Khalil in the library stacks too.
What was the point in telling you when I was the only one
seeing these things?"

"The point is that you can't just decide it's your burden

to carry alone. You can't just make these decisions for us. We're all in this now."

"You're right. I rushed into it, convinced myself it would do no good to share, so I didn't." She smiled at me and continued. "In all the weird, unexplainable things that keep happening in that room, it always goes back to my brother, who died last summer. Seeing him or hearing his voice or whatever. Ellis, maybe it's your dad who's the connector. Maybe it would be more apparent in the photos if you stepped inside the room. Devlin, you said that your wife kept talking about your son, who also died, how a lot of her odd behavior roots back to that. What if the room takes that and keeps twisting it until it's all you can see?"

"What's that Pierce Brown quote?" Ellis asked. "'Death begets death begets death'? Maybe that's all the room wants."

We all looked at one another, digesting the new connection. I should have realized sooner. Should have warned her instead of brushing it off. Sure, the warping wasn't in every photo, but I knew it was in every photo of Mira. As always, my focus was on her. I didn't even think of the others, of what could be connecting them. I flipped through the photos, going back two days.

In the photos of Mira and Ellis together, the trees swayed around her like she was the gravitational pull they bent toward. Ellis's side was more subtle, gentle in its movement.

There was no warping in the portrait of Izzy midlaugh or the ones of Elena behind the desk.

In the library, the shelves bent near Ellis but not Izzy.

On the walk home, the space around Mira, Ellis, and Devlin melted around them, stronger here than in the previous photos.

It was so obvious, I didn't know why it hadn't been our first thought. Why didn't I see it when it was literally right under my nose this whole time?

I went back to the photo of Elena. She was well lit, but the light didn't extend behind her. If this was true, why wouldn't the warping want her too? Why wouldn't it reach her the same way it touched Ellis? I zoomed in on the background, hoping to catch an edge of a swirl, but I had the aperture at f/1.4 and it was hard to see anything with the background that dark and out of focus. Maybe there was something there. But it would be impossible to be sure.

As far as we could tell, death was the only connection among the three of them. It's like the room used a guest's memories of deaths until it could absorb the guest's death, a cycle forever playing on a loop as it grew stronger each time.

"If that's true, that answers our question of how does it work," Ellis said.

"Technically, it also answers our only other question of how do we stop it," Mira said.

His brow furrowed, and he waited for her to explain.

"We can't," she finally said. He started to speak up—most likely to reassure her that there was more that could be done, that we just needed to keep at this—but stopped when he heard his name being called out in that abrupt way only a parent can do. Behind him, we saw his mom approaching, her footsteps quick and precise. Her smile seemed forced. There was real anger beneath it. You could see it in the tense lines around her eyes and in the muscle near her jaw that pulsed with every step.

He realized too late that he had the record book he had stolen this morning in clear sight. It sat there next to him, a beacon for his mother.

"Ellis, did you take that from the back room?"

Before he could even attempt a lie, she steamrollered ahead.

"This obsession isn't healthy."

"Mom, please. You don't understa—"

"No, you don't understand. Things happen. Life is dark and unfair and you're too young to grasp the fact that these things don't need a reason. They just happen. People fucking die, Ellis. This isn't going to bring him back. Nothing is going to bring him back." Ellis sat in that stunned silence, unable to say anything. We all looked at one another, mostly afraid to look in her direction. She turned her attention to Izzy. "And you, you should know better than to entertain this." This she said quieter but with the same level of fervent anger.

Izzy started to defend this, whatever *this* was, but Ellis's mom held up her hand, quickly shutting her down. It trembled a little, and she turned it to a fist back down at her side.

To Devlin she said, "I don't even know who you are, sir, but I think you should leave. You too, girls. I've let this go on for long enough. Ellis, let's go."

He didn't bother saying anything this time. He just picked up his things, mouthed "Sorry" to the group, and followed her back. We all watched as they rounded the corner and disappeared from view.

THIRTY-THREE

Mira

Izzy quickly grabbed her things and left to start her shift. Devlin followed, mumbling a quiet good night as he headed toward his room.

"Shall we?" Layla said as she stood up.

I hesitated, torn between going back to that god-forsaken room and spending more time reminding myself to breathe when I was this close to water.

"In a bit." Turns out, I'd rather know my demons.

"Okay," she said, stretching out the word. She sat back down, this time at the edge of the pool closest to me. Being on the pool chair was as close as I wanted to be to the water, but it was exhausting being scared of so many things. Maybe this was one thing I didn't have to run from.

I took off my shoes and socks and sat down next to her. I forced air into every corner of my lungs, filled them to the brim, and then released. Her eyes went wide as I dipped my legs into the cool water, letting my pants soak through. I could see the questions she wanted to ask, but instead she just smiled and squeezed my hand. I didn't think before I rubbed small circles against her palm with my thumb. Instantly, I felt her hand tense. I knew I shouldn't have. I knew it. But it felt instinctual, like my hand was a thing of its own and all it wanted was her. Even in the dim pool lighting, I could see the red in her cheeks.

"Do you want to go for a swim?" she asked, the words tumbling from her mouth. She didn't wait for me to answer. Instead, she pulled her hand away from mine and stood up.

"It's April. In Indiana. It's not exactly pool weather."

She scoffed. "Are we going to let that stop us? All I know is that it's spring break." And with that, she quickly stripped off her dress and cannonballed into the water. I barely had time to process the fact that Layla just took her dress off in front of me before the splash hit me. One fleeting moment of a black satin bra and blue underwear adorned with yellow ducks. It was too endearing not to smile at.

After a few seconds, she came up for air. Her long black hair was slicked back away from her face. Where it met the water, it fanned out in soft waves.

"It's practically warm. Not cold at all," she said, shivering.

"Okay, clearly you're lying. Come on, I'll help." I reached a hand out, but she just shook her head and swam away.

"My body just needs a second to adjust."

She dove under again, acclimating herself to the cold water. I mostly didn't want to. I didn't. I hadn't even managed to take a bath since last summer. My God, it was exhausting being this scared. I just wanted to sink beneath the surface and feel the water for all that it was. Nothing less, nothing more.

I didn't bother taking off my jumpsuit. I didn't want to give myself the chance to back out. Instead, I closed my eyes and pushed off against the ledge, sliding into the water in one seamless motion.

The water was jarring, a shock to my entire system. Beneath the surface, the world was muffled and quiet. It was almost funny knowing that, for once, I didn't need to remind myself to breathe under here. After a few seconds, I opened my eyes to find Layla underwater too. She was close, only a few inches away. Her hair danced around her in a dark cloud. She looked majestic. I wanted to reach out and touch her, to put a hand against her waist and close the distance between us. But we stayed under, let the quiet surround us as we stared at each other, neither wanting to break first. Beneath the surface, nothing above existed. Not really, anyway. We were frozen in this moment, and what we were outside of it was inconsequential. I would take this moment even if it was all she could give me.

Finally, when my lungs began to scream for air, I reached for the surface to refill them. She did too, and we just laughed for a second, a little breathless and giddy at this turn of events.

"I wasn't expecting you to join me," she said.

"I wasn't either."

"Hold on," she said before paddling toward her camera at the edge of the pool. She stretched forward, trying to reach it, then, very carefully, adjusted the settings and held it over the water. She pointed it at me, and I gave her my best model face. A little serious. A little sultry. A bit of shoulder to go along with it. She laughed and showed me the photo. The warping was still there. Muddled in the water, sure, but undeniable.

But something else was wrong too.

"Do I really look like that?"

"Like what?"

Everything about my face was wrong, and yet I couldn't nail down why. Something just felt menacing about it. The edge of a smirk, the tilt of a head. My eyes seemed to know something I didn't.

"I don't know. My face. It just— I don't look like myself."

"I must have just caught you at a weird angle," she said. She glanced at it one more time and put the camera away. Maybe she was right. Maybe all I did was look for

the bad, the dark, the shadows. I would only find what I searched for.

I floated on my back for a second, let the water do the work while I stared up at the stars. I imagined the warping in the pictures twist and turn. Weaving its way around me while I lay here on the surface. Death had to be the answer. It connected us. It fed the room. I should have known it would all come back to Khalil.

"You know, ever since he died, I've wondered how my parents would've felt if it was me." It was easier to admit certain things with the water in my ears, the world this muffled. Like I was speaking into an abyss. It could take my words if it wanted, let them disappear into the nothingness as soon as I said them. I didn't mind.

From the corner of my eye, I could see Layla was close, listening.

"Losing a son is harder on Arab parents. Not that they'd ever admit it, but it's true. It's part of the cultural DNA, you know? He's expected to be the financial support one day. He's the one they brag about. Hell, the son carries the family name. In a way, my family's branch of Hamdi died with him." I stood up to look at her. She just looked back. She didn't try to tell me that I was wrong or that I was crazy to think that. She understood. When no one else did, she always understood.

"I remember reading this article or post or whatever about how immigrant parents experience this phenomenon of being frozen in time and lost to time," she said. "They carry with them the values that existed the year they left their home country and spend decades enforcing traditions that technically don't even exist anymore. Not in the way they're convinced they do. Their country moves on and grows and evolves without them. Then they go back for a visit and are thrown off by how different everything is back home. Suddenly they belong neither here nor there. But it only makes them hold on to what they know tighter. It's like a ship without a sail. You keep heading north as much as you can when north is all you know." She moved her hands along the surface of the water, gently, like she was afraid to tear it. "There are some things they can't shake. No matter how badly you want them to." She didn't look at me when she said that part, just down toward the ripples we were making in the water, and I wondered if she was referring to something specific, something secret and hers alone that maybe I wasn't privy to.

"I get it. When I came out, they acted like I betrayed them. Like queer kids were synonymous with America, tainted by Western influences. My mom is convinced things would have been different if we never came to this country."

Layla rolled her eyes and laughed. It was one harsh,

quick laugh. Nothing about this was surprising to either of us.

I floated on my back for a bit, let the water mute the rest of the world while I stared up at the night sky. That's why I wasn't sure if I heard Layla say what she said next.

"What?"

She hesitated, picking at a stray leaf that was floating on the surface. She crunched it up in her palm and threw it a few feet away. A look of soft determination washed over her face when she met my eyes.

"I just mean that when you came out, it was like a puzzle piece fitting into a perfectly shaped space. Of course you were bi. I don't think any part of me was surprised. I just wondered, why not me?"

"It was always you." She froze in the water, but there was no going back now. "Of course I thought about us. I'd be crazy not to. But you're straight, and what we have is too good for me to mess up. You're my best friend, Layla. That's all that matters to me."

She looked like she wanted to say something, like words were resting on the tip of her tongue, if only she spoke them into existence, but maybe this was all wishful thinking. Here was an opening. Here was me shoving the door wide open, but anything I saw in her possibly liking me back was me projecting. I saw what I wanted, and all I saw was her.

She smiled but didn't say anything. I wasn't sure what I would say if I were her either. She was only a few inches away now, and when she glanced at my lips, I forgot how to breathe. As if I were still underwater and there was no air to be found. My eyes quickly flashed to her mouth and back to her eyes, only to find her watching me. I wanted to be wrong. I wanted to edge closer, to lean into her and believe that she would meet me halfway. I took a step forward and she didn't back away.

Before either of us could take another step, a breeze ran through the water, sending ripples all the way down. We both shivered when it reached us.

"Should we head back?" she asked.

"Yeah," I said, backing away. Why didn't I think anything through? Why did I have to be so reckless with our friendship?

"This was probably not my best idea. Let's get out of here." We swam toward the ladder and hoisted ourselves up. Layla grabbed her dress and quickly threw it on. I barely had time to look away before she was dressed again. I grabbed my shoes and we walked back to the room. Slowly, the feelings of floating and release flitted away. In their place was dread. I could feel my heartbeat against my chest. The closer we were, the faster it was.

I hated all of this. How walking back made me aware of the heavy pit in my stomach, how hopeless we all felt. How it quickly overwhelmed every other feeling I'd contained only a moment ago. How much power I'd given this room. Fuck this room.

I walked faster toward it. Sure, I couldn't deny the fact that my heart beat louder with every step I took, but I would keep walking.

"You know, after everything we learned, maybe we should stay somewhere else, see if that bed-and-breakfast can take us," Layla said as we stood in front of the door. It was tempting, Layla's offer. But no. I was tired of running away. Of keeping a safe distance when we now knew there was no such thing.

"No, I need to do this. If it wants death, it's going to have to kill me first," I joked.

"I know, Mira. That's what I'm worried about."

"You know what I mean. I'm going to be fine. I just can't let it get to me. I don't think this is something I can run from."

Layla decided not to push and stepped inside. My shoe landed on soggy carpet. I could hear it squish against the ground, knew that if I knelt down it would be wet and cold. I took another step and it was gone. The carpet, bone dry. Like I had imagined it all to begin with. I closed my eyes. Breathed in through my nose. Out through my mouth. I wouldn't let this room wind its way through my mind.

"Make sure to lock the door. Don't need Devlin coming in here again," Layla joked as I closed the door behind us.

"I don't know. I kind of get it? It's this room," I said, looking around. "This place doesn't feel rational. I think he was just desperate for answers. Obviously, he went about it the wrong way, but I think he's harmless. Sad. But harmless."

She didn't say anything, and my mind crept back to the walls around me.

"What do you think of him?" I said, eager to focus on anything but those walls. "I feel like we haven't gotten a second alone all day. Hard to talk shit when the people we'd talk shit about are right there."

"I don't know. Something isn't sitting right with me," she said.

"What do you mean?"

"I like him fine. I just don't trust him."

"Why? Do you think he's hiding something, like he hasn't told us everything?"

She bit her lip, thinking it over. "I don't know. It's just a feeling. Whatever. We'll be gone tomorrow."

I took that as the best opening I was going to get.

"Actually, I was thinking. What if we stayed another day? Told our parents the car wasn't ready and spent the day here? It's too late to go to Chicago, anyway, so we could round back to Michigan and go home from here instead." I wasn't sure how she'd react, but I knew that leaving now felt incomplete. If we looked at the data more, maybe tried to get in contact with past guests, tried to figure out whatever missing piece we had left, I could leave better prepared for what was to come.

"What good would that do? If you ask me, the sooner we put this place behind us, the better."

"Just seems like there's more we can learn about this place. Something we're not seeing." I didn't know how to explain that if we left now, I'd spend the rest of my life thinking about Room 9, trying my best to convince myself it wasn't what I remembered and inevitably making my way back here for answers. Answers I could find now if only we stayed a little while longer. I knew this in my bones, knew it as fact.

Layla thought about it for a second and went for the compromise. "Let's sleep on it and see how we feel in the morning. We'll talk to the group and go from there, okay?"

I nodded and sat on the floor, not wanting to ruin the sheets with my wet jumpsuit. She went to the bathroom to shower and change and came back out a few minutes later. It wasn't late, barely nine, but I hadn't actually slept last night, and I was exhausted. A shower sounded like a dream right now. Hot, almost scalding water. Strong pressure. Shampoo. And the fact that I'd run the last two mornings without showering after was starting to feel gross. Sink showers could only get me so far.

"I think I'm going to take a shower."

I said it before I even really decided it, but I'd committed to it now. Quick shower. Face the beast and all that. This feeling wasn't going anywhere, and avoiding it only made me feel like I was lying to myself. Pretending wouldn't make any of this go away. Maybe I couldn't wash off this weighty uneasiness I had in the room, but I'd feel better knowing I faced a small part of it anyway.

"You sure? I know you've been avoiding the bathroom. Not that I blame you. I just—" She paused, hesitating. "I just don't want you to be alone if you don't have to be."

"What are you going to do? Watch me shower?" I said, trying to lighten the mood. But her eyes went wide for half a second, and she looked away.

"It's all right. I'll be out in five minutes." It was difficult to explain, to understand, but something in me knew that the farther I tried to run, the heavier it felt. Like it could feed on fear and avoidance. I needed to face this head-on. At least for five minutes.

"Okay. I have to call my mom anyway. Reassure her we have not been kidnapped and left for dead in the middle of nowhere."

"Best of luck with that. I'm happy to send her a picture of you with today's newspaper if she asks for proof of life."

She rolled her eyes and took out her phone.

I hadn't even reached the bathroom door before I heard her mom yelling on the other end in Arabic. We didn't understand each other's dialects perfectly, but I understood enough to know this was not going to be a fun call for her.

"All right. Shower time. Let's do this," I said to myself. I closed the door behind me, made sure I had towels at the ready and my shampoo and conditioner within reach.

I peeled off my wet clothes, piled them near the door, and slid the glass shower door open. It was the same feeling of being convinced you needed to look under your bed because you knew, just knew, that there was a man with a knife under there, and every second you sat in bed paralyzed was a second you were leaving yourself vulnerable. I stepped onto the cold tile and closed the shower door behind me, making sure to look around the small space first. If something was lying in wait, it wouldn't surprise me. It was ridiculous. I knew that. But the feelings felt real, and I needed to face them like they were.

The water could have been hotter, but the pressure was great, and I stood beneath it as it beat down on my shoulders for a long while. I closed my eyes and tried to think of every shitty thing that happened inside this room, imagined it all circling the drain and making its way down. I could do this. I could survive this room. Maybe it wasn't a question of strength but of resolve. If I said it enough times, I could will it into truth.

By the time I opened my eyes again, the water was at my ankles. I checked the faucet, but the drain was set to open, so it didn't make sense. I tried to quickly rinse out the shampoo from my hair, but something was clearly wrong. The water was at my knees now, filling up faster than it could possibly be coming out of the showerhead. For a split second, I thought about the inevitable flood I'd create by opening the door and decided to do it anyway.

I pulled the handle, but it didn't budge.

The water quickly rose to my waist.

THIRTY-FOUR

The water is quick and steady.

Mira does not understand how the small space can fill up so fast, how it can fill up at all. But it is at her shoulders now, and she is screaming for help. The word slips out in Arabic, and it surprises even her.

Swiftly, the water rises, muffling her screams. She pounds on the glass with one hand. The other pulls at the latch to no avail.

Mira takes a second to think, to collect her thoughts before there are none to collect. Her earlier confidence is a distant memory now.

As the water covers her head, Mira understands who is in control. She swims up and takes one expansive breath, fills her lungs as taut as they will allow. Soon, there is no more air for her to steal.

She swims and pounds and pulls and wonders why the soapy water filling her mouth tastes of salt.

THIRTY-FIVE

Layla

I wasn't sure what I heard at first. I set my phone down and tried to listen. It was muffled and inconsistent. I thought it was the neighbors, but it took me too long to realize it was coming from the bathroom.

"Mom, let me call you back," I said.

"You better, Layla. Or so help me, Allah."

I hung up and put my ear against the door.

"Mira, everything okay?"

The thudding became louder, faster. I turned the handle, but of course it was locked. I ran to my bag to grab a quarter and twisted the narrow crevice in the lock until the handle released. Mira was behind the shower glass, her fists pounding on the door. I pulled open the shower door, expecting it to be broken, the metal hinges stuck or the latch having fallen off, but it opened with ease. Mira tumbled out, falling to her knees on the cold tile. I wrapped her in a towel as she gasped for breath, trying to take in all the air she could. I gave her a second to breathe before I brushed the hair away from her face.

"You're okay, you're okay." I kept repeating it until she seemed to believe me. "What happened?"

She waited awhile before speaking. "The shower. It kept filling up with water. It was over my head. I couldn't—I couldn't breathe." Her voice was hoarse, each word like sandpaper against her throat. We both looked back at the shower, the water still running overhead. It all went down the drain. Nothing had come spilling out when I opened the door, but I had to remind myself that that didn't mean she didn't feel what she felt. It didn't mean that she didn't think she was going to die. We still didn't fully understand how this room worked, but if Mira was convinced she couldn't breathe, then maybe she could have died if I hadn't come in when I did. This room was pure darkness. It was rot and ruin and wrong, and Mira was drowning in it. I would help her find whatever light there was to find even if I had to drag her out of here myself.

I didn't care what was happening. I didn't care what was real and what wasn't. I didn't care if this room was possessed or haunted or was something outside of our understanding. Only one thing mattered, and I was looking at her.

"All right, we're done with this place. I know you want to see this through, but we're not doing that at the cost of your life. Whatever you feel about this room, it's stronger inside of it. So, we're getting out of here. Okay?"

She looked at me for a second, glanced back at the shower, and nodded.

"Great, get dressed. We're going to go get your car back."

"It's late. We don't even know if the garage is open," she said.

"We're going to bang on the door until Bob or whatever his name is wakes up and opens the garage. I'm going to go see if Izzy can drive us."

"Wait," she said, grabbing my hand. The blood vessels in her eyes had popped. She looked tired and scared, and I didn't know what to do for her. "Can we go together? I—I don't want to be alone right now."

Her soft, pleading eyes. How tightly she gripped my hand. It broke my fucking heart. "Of course, take your time. I'm here."

She pulled the towel tighter around herself and left the bathroom. I pulled the shower handle again, toying with it, testing it, but it worked perfectly. The door moved back and forth seamlessly. None of this made sense. None of it. But it was finally dawning on me that it didn't need to. It was as real as anything else. Mira was in danger. I didn't need proof to be convinced of that.

I waited a moment before I followed, wanting to give

her a minute of privacy while she changed. She was dressed in black jeans and a dark green hoodie with leather detailing up the arms. She stuck her phone and important cards into her back pockets, grabbed the motel keys, and switched back to her black combats.

"Should we take our things with us?" I asked. Our stuff was littered around the room, but it wouldn't take that long to shove it all into a suitcase. She thought for a second, deliberating between doing it now or coming back for it.

"Yeah, let's get this over with." She started throwing things in her duffel. Shoes on top of T-shirts on top of jeans. I grabbed everything I could find. It didn't matter if it was hers or mine. I just forced it into my suitcase and zipped it closed.

"Ready?" I asked.

She took in the room one last time. I wasn't sure if she was checking for things we missed or wanted one last look at this place before we left for good. She grabbed her leather jacket, threw the duffel bag strap over her shoulder, and nodded.

I grabbed my things and we went to find Izzy.

She was reading behind the front desk, her feet up on the counter, when we walked in.

"Ladies, this is a nice surprise," she said, smiling at us.

"Would you be able to drive us to the mechanic?

Something's happened and we can't stay the night," I said. Mira placed the motel keys on the counter but didn't say anything.

"Oh God." Izzy dropped her feet from the desk. They landed with a thud against the hardwood floor.

Ellis came down right then, skipping every other step.

"I got your text," he said to Mira. "What happened? Are you both okay?" His eyes danced between us, waiting for answers.

I looked at Mira, unsure if she wanted me to say something or if she would. After a few seconds, she spoke.

"I was in the shower and I thought I was drowning. The door wouldn't open and it filled up with water. I couldn't breathe. I'm sorry, but I can't stay here. I just really want to grab my car."

Izzy looked at us both for a second, her brows knitting together with concern. I could tell this wasn't about whether she believed us or not. It wasn't about the room or what was inside it. She was in problem-solving mode. She might have only known us for two days, but it was clear she was worried. I would have thought it was sort of sweet if I wasn't so focused on the situation at hand.

"I can take you guys to my place, if you'd like? Just for the night, and we can figure something out in the morning," she offered.

"You're welcome to stay in my room, if you want?" Ellis interjected. We looked at each other, contemplating.

"No, I think I've had enough of this town. No offense," Mira said with a small smile.

"Trust me, none taken." Ellis smiled, but he looked sad as he did it.

"Thank you for everything," Mira said. She wrapped her arms around his waist in a tight hug. He froze for a second and returned it, resting his arms around her shoulders. They stayed like that for a second, her head resting on his chest until she stepped back.

"Text me, okay?" he said as he looked at her, his hands on her shoulders. She smiled and nodded.

"It was nice meeting you," he said as he turned to me. He hesitated for a second, then hugged me too. Quick and awkward but still sweet. His chin rested on my head for a second before he let go. Maybe I'd miss him after we left this place. Just a little.

Izzy pulled her keys from the front pocket of her jeans and grabbed her messenger bag.

"Okay, let's go."

We walked to her car, parked outside the office. Izzy made her way around while Mira pushed down the passenger seat and jumped in the back, taking my suitcase with her. She shoved the seat forward and I took shotgun.

"I'm not sure if Bill is going to be there, but if he isn't, I know James, so just let me do the talking," Izzy said. We didn't protest.

After a moment, Izzy said, "I'm glad you had a chance to say goodbye to Elly. He would have been crushed if he didn't get to."

She looked a little longer at Mira through the rearview mirror when she said this, and it was nice to feel a little validated that maybe Ellis did have a crush on her after all. That I wasn't the only one who saw it.

"We would have been too," Mira said

We drove in silence the rest of the way. Izzy had made another attempt or two at conversation, but it was clear that Mira didn't feel like talking. I couldn't blame her. I was emotionally and physically exhausted. At this point, all I wanted was for us to be on the road, making our way back home. Who knew I'd be looking forward to seeing my family by the end of this trip?

As we drove up, we could see that the light was on. There was classical music coming from the garage, something fast and elaborate. Notes climbing after one another as they reached for a crescendo. It wasn't what I would have imagined for Bill, but I liked knowing it.

Mira and I got out of the car, and Izzy followed us.

"You don't have to come. You've helped more than

enough by getting us here," I said as I pulled my suitcase out of the back seat. Mira was already standing next to me with her backpack on and duffel strapped across her body.

"I can't leave two girls at the end of a road by themselves in the middle of the night. Let me just make sure that you two get your car."

"Thanks," Mira said softly, and smiled at her.

"Of course." She put her arms around us both. "Now, let's get your baby back."

We walked toward the open garage. A few lights were turned on, but most of it looked dim. There were a couple cars parked inside, Mira's included, and beneath one of them we could see someone's grease-stained coveralls peeking out. The sound of a wrench clanging against metal echoed. Mira knocked on the hood of the car.

"Sorry, we're closed," the voice said.

"Come on, Jamie. You're really going to turn us away without a glance? Your customer service reviews must be shit."

The sound of metal against metal stopped. For a single second, James didn't move. And then, he slid away from beneath the car, took one look at Izzy, and his face broke out into a stupid grin.

"Izzy!"

He stood up, wiped his hands on his coveralls, and went

to hug her, making sure to keep his hands away from her clothes, just in case. He was taller than her but not by much. His dark hair was buzzed low to his scalp, and there were dark smudges on his cheek. I couldn't help but notice the single tattoo on his left forearm, a black band against dark skin peeking through the edge of his rolled-up sleeve.

"It's been a while. How's the old Ford Focus treating you?"

"It got us here, so well enough."

They looked at each other for a few seconds, both smiling, both making us feel awkward for just standing there.

"Ah yes, we are here because they left their car with you, and we're hoping we can grab it now instead of tomorrow."

"Sorry, guys. No can do, I'm not allowed to process out the cars. I just fix 'em. Bill handles the rest; you can talk to him first thing in the morning though," he said.

To his credit, he did look genuinely apologetic, but a lot of good that did us. He could keep his sorry. We'd rather take the car.

"Jamie, come on. You can't do an old friend a favor?" Izzy said, pouting. She was laying it on thick. Mira and I looked at each other, seeing through it, but Jamie was melted butter in her hands. Already, he was hesitating.

"Which one?" he asked, looking at both of us.

"The Chrysler Sebring? 2004," Mira said.

"I—I don't know. The airbags haven't been replaced yet, and I didn't get a chance to reset the airbag module. Bill will be pissed if he realizes it's gone in the morning."

"Tell him we insisted," she said. And then her smile dropped, dropping the nice girl act along with it. "And we are. Insisting."

"Iz, come on."

"Don't Iz me."

"I could get fired!"

"You're like Bill's second son. He'd never fire you."

"You don't know that," he said. His arms were crossed. His eyes narrowed.

"I'm willing to take my chances."

They stared at each other for a few seconds, both waiting for the other to break. Until Mira decided for them. To my left I could see that she had been inching toward the wall of keys this whole time. She glanced at James, pocketed the keys, and tiptoed to her car.

James barely had time to react before he heard the engine. I could see the adrenaline and panic coursing through her from here. As shocked as I wanted to be, this had Mira written all over it. But who could blame her? These were desperate times.

"I'm sorry! I'm really sorry!" she screamed as she began

to drive off. She didn't say anything to me, but her eyes were wide as she leaned forward to open the passenger door and motioned for me to get in. I looked back at James and Izzy. His jaw had fallen open as he stood frozen in place. Izzy looked absolutely delighted. She winked at me, and that was all I needed. I jumped in, suitcase and all, and closed the door behind me.

"Whoa, whoa. Not cool, guys!" James yelled after us. He started jogging toward the car, but Mira floored it out of there before he could reach us. The windows were open, and I could hear Izzy laughing. From the rearview mirror, she waved us off as James slid his hands through his buzzed hair. She put an arm over his shoulder, and I could see him relax a bit, his shoulders lowered, his hands at his sides. He might have been mad, but a second later, he was smiling at something Izzy said.

"Text Izzy that I'll send her money for the car tomorrow."

I threw the suitcase in the back seat, took out my phone, and shot off a text to Izzy. All of this was totally fine. Totally. Was it even stealing if we planned to pay? More importantly, was it stealing if it was our own car?

"I can't believe I just did that," Mira said after a few seconds.

"I can."

We looked at each other, the adrenaline coursing through us both, and laughed. An unbridled sort of laugh, and God, it felt good.

"Ready?" she asked, a little breathless.

"Let's get the hell out of here."

THIRTY-SIX

Mira

"Do you want to grab milkshakes or something before we start the drive back?" I said. I knew a part of me was worried about how I'd feel when I left this town, when I put distance between me and the room. I worried about what I would do if nothing changed, if there really was no leaving it behind. I knew she knew it too, but Layla didn't question it. She didn't call me out on it or push me until I broke. Leaving was inevitable, but at least she'd give me the time I needed to be ready.

Instead, she said, "A milkshake is exactly what I need right now. Yes, please."

We pulled into the diner. It was almost midnight, and I was glad they were open twenty-four hours. The place was mostly empty except for a handful of groups scattered throughout. We could sit, waste as much time as possible, dreading what we were heading toward.

Or I could get this over with.

"Can you order a chocolate shake for me? We can get them to go. I just need to go to the bathroom."

She nodded and went to place our order.

The bathroom was dim and cramped, only meant for one person. I needed a minute. One minute to breathe and collect my thoughts. I felt like I was made of tidal waves held back at their peak. Like I was wavering between falling and being and I didn't know how to do either. What did Neil Gaiman always say? If you can't do something, pretend to be someone who can? I looked into the mirror, trying to convince myself. I could be that Mira. I could get in that car and leave Room 9 behind me. I needed to believe I could. I bent down toward the sink and splashed cold water on my face. My cheeks were flushed and my hair looked frantic, slowly drying in every direction. But my eyes were determined. I looked like myself.

And then I didn't.

I hadn't blinked, but in a single second my eyes were looking back at me differently, menacingly. The same way they were in Layla's photo. Something had shifted. I didn't recognize what I saw. The reflection took a small step back, straightened her shoulders, just slightly, and opened her mouth.

"Come closer," she whispered. My mind flashed back to my brother, to me saying the same words and convincing him to leave shallow waters behind, and I knew then there was no escaping any of this. I couldn't run home to safety when there was no safety to run to. This was all I had going forward.

The fear inside my heart and the bile in my throat.

She said it again, this time with a bend of a hand, inviting me in. I couldn't look away, couldn't break eye contact. It felt impossible to, like I was connected to her in this eerie and awful way. But I also knew that I needed to, like my life depended on it.

My hand found the door handle. I closed my eyes and pushed down. I couldn't see her, but I could feel her, could smell the sunscreen on her skin and the salt water in her hair. I knew she was watching me go, her hand still outstretched in midair, but I slammed the door behind me and rested my back against it. As if I needed to trap her in there. I focused on my breathing, the expansion of my lungs. The release of my chest.

In.

Out.

"Everything okay?"

The adrenaline from earlier had waned, and all that was left was fear to take its place. I opened my eyes to find Layla holding two shakes, concern etched on her face.

I nodded, took my shake from her hand, and headed out, hoping she was following.

There was no escaping this. It didn't matter how far we ran or how fast. Even if we never stopped running, this room had clawed its way onto my back, and I was naïve to think I could win. At least not like this. We needed to go back. Needed to put an end to this once and for all. I couldn't leave without knowing I had tried.

I got in the driver's seat and slammed the door behind me. Layla followed, but I could feel her hesitance.

"You sure you're okay?" she asked as she gently set her shake in one of the cupholders between us.

"We have to go back." I glanced at her, worried about her reaction. For one quick second, she laughed. Then she saw my face.

"You're kidding," she said, deadpan.

I didn't say anything. I just stared straight ahead and focused on the road.

"Mira. An hour ago, you thought you were going to die. Why would we go back?"

"Because I never left that room. Not really."

She softened a bit and reached out a hand. "We're going to figure this out. I promise." She squeezed my hand resting on the gear shift between us and my heart beat faster for an entirely different reason. "I just don't think going back is the answer."

"Please. I have to. Or I'm just going to keep running from something I have no chance of beating."

She was quiet for a minute, and then: "What are you planning to do?"

"Finish it."

The rest of the drive back was short and quiet. Layla sipped her strawberry shake in silence, and I appreciated her not trying to get more out of me. In all honesty, I wasn't entirely sure what my plan was either. All I knew was leaving wasn't it. My chocolate shake sat there, the plastic cup sweating as beads of water traveled down to the cupholder. I didn't have the heart or the stomach to touch it.

I drove down the tree-lined path toward the motel and forced myself to breathe. The closer I drove to Room 9, the louder my heart beat. I was so sure Layla could hear and was just being nice enough not to point it out.

As much as I wanted to vomit at the thought of setting foot inside, what I did next was barely a choice. A part of this room was a part of me. The mirror at the diner proved as much.

I slammed the brakes once we got to the parking lot and jumped out of the car. I didn't care that the keys were still in the ignition, that the door was left wide open. I just followed the car beams that lit up Room 9's door on the far side of the motel, with Layla close behind me. Devlin was a few feet away, in front of his own room, lighting a cigarette, when he saw me coming. He paused for a second, the cigarette at his lips, the metal lighter frozen in place. I could see the confusion in his eyes where the flame lit their edges. He didn't stop me when I grabbed the lighter from his hand. I could feel his eyes on me as I strode toward the room, but he stayed where he was, watching us. The door was ajar, only an inch or so, but I didn't remember leaving it open when we left. I heard the click of Layla's camera next to me. I glanced at her and she mumbled, "Sorry," and started to put it away, but then she paused and turned the display toward me.

We stared at the photo, stunned at what had appeared. On the screen, the door was framed in the center. At the opening, the warping leaked out. Like it was oozing at the seams. We were nearing the room, only steps away now, and I could feel it looming over us. It was heavy and dark. The room couldn't contain it all. I didn't need the photo to know that it seeped out of the open doorway and tugged. *Come*, it seemed to whisper. We looked at each other and then toward the door. I wasn't backing out now.

One last time, I stepped into Room 9.

FRIDAY

THIRTY-SEVEN

Ellis has one hand poised over the door. He knocks once, hesitates, puts his hand back in his pocket, and considers walking away. Instead, he looks up at the golden nine hanging just off center and waits for the gray door to open. For months, the room could feel his guilt grow heavy, could taste the way it simmered below his surface, wanting to consume him, delicious and untouchable. But Ellis is smart and, up until now, has stayed away. Tonight, after months of pulling and tugging and wrenching, Ellis finds himself caught by the edge of a perpetual hook.

"Ellis, what are you doing here?" Mira says. Mira understands what happens here. Understands why he's never stepped inside until now. But Ellis is engulfed by the part he's played in this room's history. Is overwhelmed by his own remorse and culpability. Is convinced that there are some things he must answer for.

The room yawns open to him, and Ellis steps inside.

Yes, he knows certain answers lie behind this door, and facing what scares him most is the only way to truly understand. Especially after having spent hours engrossed in this room's history, unable to deny all the people he had allowed to set foot in this room. But if Ellis is honest with himself, this isn't why he decides to go inside. Though even atonement can be self-serving. Still. Atone he must.

Ellis thinks of Gretchen, the elderly woman who was on her way to surprise her daughter a few weeks back. He remembers the sound of her laugh and the deep smile lines etched onto her face when he checked her in. He thinks of Sam, a man not much older than him, who seemed quiet and kind and had only stayed for one night. Ellis thinks of all the others he checked in himself, even after he had connected the dots of Room 9's history when his dad died four months ago. Every name that, earlier today, turned up a search result he would never forget. So many were dead. None of them had to be.

Finally, Ellis answers the siren call.

It is all I need.

"I saw you guys come back," he begins to say, but quickly the words fade. He is silent by the last word. He notices the lighter in her hands but does not have time to question it. Ellis is breathless at the weight of it all, at the overwhelming guilt and shame and death that skewers him in the stomach now that he is inside.

Some people take days. Take dreams and secrets and objects left behind. They take prying and patience. But little Elly has always been a part of this room from afar.

He is brought to his knees by the certainty of it all. He knows that every time he checked someone into this room, he willingly risked their life, and the guilt of it could swallow him whole. His heart is being gripped; he is sure of it. Ellis looks up and instantly knows that this is a mistake.

Inches from his face are the feet of a woman who died in 1990. Her body hangs limp above Ellis. It gently sways from where it is attached by a brown belt around the fan. She wears a navy dress that grazes the rotting flesh of her toes. Ellis knows this is Lola even if he does not dare look up. Her photo hangs on the inside of his closet, the second death listed there. Ellis crawls back, trying to get away from her body, only to touch another. He looks down to see his hand has landed on long, slender fingers. It is Maya. Her torso drapes back over the edge of Mira's bed. Her neck bends at an unnatural angle against the floor, the skin paper-thin and tinted purple. Maya's dead, swollen eyes look back at him.

Ellis knows that if he looks up and to the left, he will see a body on the other bed, Eugene's. Knows that near the bathroom rests Amir, who handcuffed himself to the radiator and subsequently starved himself to death. The putrid stench sticks to the back of his throat, and it takes all of Ellis to swallow back the bile that rises.

He knows all seven bodies are here, with Sadie's eighth floating on the pool's surface. Ellis does not need to count. Ellis does not need to make his way to the bathroom to know that he will find his father facedown, along with Peter and Marianna, their bodies draped over each other on the tile. He is thankful for a small, fleeting moment that he cannot see inside the bathroom from where he is.

He feels their pain and anguish roiling inside him.

Ellis finally understands that these walls know him better than anyone. They've called to him for months, and as time went by, the cries became louder. And today, now that he's spent a day submerged in the extensive damage he knows he's had a hand in causing, including the crushing realization that he had checked in Devlin's wife himself, he knows he has no choice but to give in to the Pull. Ellis understands that he had no hand in the eight deaths of this room. Some were before he was even born, the rest before he understood the history of Room 9. But it does not matter. He knows they are only emblematic of the damage he has caused since he learned what this room was capable of—how he failed to steer people away. The room would not be so well fed without him handing over the keys to each victim. Eight deaths only signify the others to come.

Ellis can pretend to be the hero, but deep down, he knows it is a lie. He still gave this room to guests when he felt he had no choice. He did have one though. He always did. He chose living with the guilt of letting everyone die. And even though it was a more complicated decision than that, it is all it boils down to.

He pulls himself up. Ellis knows that he's figured it out, the key to what makes me twist and turn, to what makes me salivate for more, what is behind the hunger that pulls at strangers, but in return for this newfound knowledge, Ellis does not know if he is prepared to pay the price. This place has sunk its teeth into him. There is no letting go.

THIRTY-EIGHT

Layla

Ellis was on his knees, his fingers woven into the carpet. His breathing was shallow and stilted, but after a few seconds, he stood up and looked at Mira. His eyes were unfocused, like he was trying his best not to look behind her.

"It's guilt. Guilt is what brings you here and it's what keeps you here."

"What? How do you know that?"

"I just do. You have to trust me. The second I walked in here, it hit me." His voice was low and ragged like it hurt to say anything. He carefully sat down on the edge of the bed and picked at his hands. "I've blamed myself for a lot, but most of all for not doing enough to stop people from coming in here. This room craves guilt, and I've got plenty to spare."

"But it doesn't make any sense. The room wants nothing to do with me, and I have things to be guilty about, things I haven't told anyone." I could feel Mira looking at me, but I kept my focus on Ellis. I thought of every time my feelings for Mira had forced me to question what I was—and hide it from everyone in my life—of how my parents would react if I ever told them.

Of how I felt every time we touched.

Of that almost kiss earlier tonight, if only I hadn't pulled away.

Of Mira.

But deep down I knew any guilt or shame I carried had nothing to do with who I was and everything to do with not being brave enough to tell her.

"No," Ellis said. "Not like . . . not like Mira."

"What does Mira have to be guilty about?" I asked.

They looked at each other, quiet for a moment, as Mira nervously flicked the lighter on and off. Ellis decided for them.

"Khalil. Mira thinks she's responsible for his death." He said the name with that hard *K* and it killed me a little that this white boy who couldn't even pronounce her brother's name knew something about Mira that I didn't.

"What is he talking about, Mira?"

I watched the emotions wash over her face. First scared. Then hesitant, wavering on a precipice. Finally, resolute.

THIRTY-NINE

Mira

I couldn't shake the feeling that if I told Layla the truth, everything would change.

But maybe it needed to.

"I didn't know how to tell you. I didn't know how to tell anyone. Telling Ellis just felt easier than telling you."

"It's not about that," Layla said, waving it off. She still looked hurt, but she powered through. "We can talk about how I didn't know any of this later. But you can't possibly think you killed your brother, can you? None of that was your fault," she told me, and I wanted to believe her. Really, I did.

"You weren't there," I said. "You don't know what I did. You wouldn't look at me the same if you knew. I couldn't tell you that I was the one who told him to come where he wasn't safe. I couldn't tell you that when the water took us farther out than we planned, he fought for air. And I definitely couldn't tell you how in my panic, I pushed my own brother under until it was too late." My eyes were trained on hers. I wouldn't look away from her. Not now. My hands shook as I flicked the lighter on and off. I hated every part of this, every word that came out of my mouth. But as loud as my guilt and shame felt, a part of me was relieved at not having to keep this from the world. A little part of me breathed a little easier. Whatever happened next was out of my hands, and there was contentment in that.

"I couldn't let you look at me like you didn't recognize me, like you wanted nothing to do with me. *I* wanted nothing to do with me." My eyes fell to my shoes.

"Don't you get it?" she said, grabbing my arms and forcing me to look up at her. "That can never happen. You were only trying to survive. You didn't even sit and think for a second that it might not be your fault. You just believed it. I love you, Mira. My God, I've loved you for so long. Nothing can change that." She whispered it. It wasn't this loud proclamation of love. No, it was tender and vulnerable and ready to be broken.

I leaned forward and I kissed her. I had imagined this moment a hundred times, thought of how I'd cradle her jaw with my hand, how my thumb would rest on her cheekbone and my other hand her waist. I thought about how she'd smell like a mix of citrus shampoo and jasmine perfume, always so sweet and encompassing when we hugged.

For a moment, she was completely still. Before I had a chance to worry that I had misunderstood what she said, Layla was kissing me back. Her lips were soft and strong and I melted into them. I melted into them a hundred times over.

Everything I felt for Layla, for this moment, was mixed with this sense of relief of being able to breathe for the first time in a year. For the first time since that moment in the sea. Guilt lives best in secret, and here was mine for the world to see.

I could feel the tears down my cheeks.

At the edge of it, I could taste our kiss turn to rust.

Layla leaned back and she looked afraid. Of me or for me, I wasn't sure. She reached out and wiped the tear from the corner of my lips.

Her thumb came back red.

FORTY

Mira is on the edge, balancing on a tightrope that, if she falls, will leave her plunging into an abyss. But then she is pulled back from the brink, left on firm ground. No one has pushed back in quite this way before. Her guilt is waning. The darkness inside her begins to leak out, begins to disappear into nothing. And all this prying and pulling will have gone to waste.

No.

The Pull works its kind of magic, strokes the fear in Mira and lets it fill up space. When the other girl sees the blood in Mira's eyes, watches it trail down her cheeks, she is horrified.

When Mira realizes what is happening, she is too. Neither notices as the open lighter falls from Mira's hand. The flame catches on the edge of the bedspread, and the smell of burnt cotton begins to fill the room. But the girl is too focused on Mira. Too distracted to realize what's at stake here. This room is burning and no one sees. Soon it will be too late.

Before Mira has a chance to wipe the blood from her face or quell the building fire around her, she falls into a sudden sort of sleep. Darkness meets her on the other side. The brain is both malleable and fragile, a dangerous combination. Mira thinks she is underwater, believes that soon her lungs will fill, is convinced that they are burning, and so they do. Mira drowns, and then the process begins again.

Water.

Burning.

Drowning.

Water.

The girl says, "Take me, damn it." But I do not want her. I only want guilt and shame and the darkness that seeps out.

FORTY-ONE
Layla

There were feelings that had quietly rested in the pit of my soul for years, feelings I didn't have words for, or the willingness to put words to. And now, here, suddenly, it was like they filled my mouth, waiting to be spoken aloud. How long had I been holding my breath, waiting for this moment and unwilling to do anything about it? There was so much I was still questioning. The only thing I was sure of was Mira.

I leaned back when I tasted the blood on the corner of her lips. She didn't seem to notice at first. She looked at me, smiling, while I followed the trail of blood up to her eyes. I reached out and touched my thumb to the corner of her mouth where the blood had collected. It was warm to the touch.

She raised her hand to wipe the blood from her face, but before she could, her eyes rolled back and she crumpled to the floor.

"Mira? Mira, what's going on? Wake up." I shook her, trying to snap her out of it. She lay completely still. I checked for a pulse. It was there, faint but evident. Her chest, though, did not move. I kept waiting for it to rise and fall, but it didn't. It was like she was holding her breath. She began to shake, like she was struggling to tear herself away from something and failing. Then, just as suddenly, her body calmed down and she was still again. That wasn't any better though. If it wasn't for her pulse, she could have been—no. I didn't even want to finish the thought.

It started again.

It was this room. Everything was this room.

"Take me, damn it," I pleaded, but Mira's body only continued to shake.

I looked up and only then remembered that Ellis was still there. He was frozen in place, watching Mira's writhing body.

"I smell smoke." Devlin appeared at the doorway, his eyes quickly landing on Mira. "What's going on?"

I had never been so thankful to see an almost-doctor in all my life.

FORTY-TWO

Mira

There is water inside every inch of me. My lungs are made of fire.

I am in water and I am not. There is drowning inside of me. Somewhere deep and painful and unreachable. But here, the darkness is all there is. I see the same endless black stretching in every direction. I know I am inside whatever makes Room 9 what it is. I know this with the same clarity we understand dreams. Sudden and sure.

There is no voice, no whispers.

Only truth.

In the distance, a figure forms. Hazy at first, but the closer I get, the clearer it becomes.

Suddenly, I am face-to-face with Khalil. He is wearing the same dark blue swimming shorts as that day. They are damp, and I can see a small puddle forming around his feet. There is no middle to this endless abyss, and yet, I know he stands at the center of it. His brown eyes go wide as he claws at his throat. Gently at first and then harder, sharper, his fingernails leaving thin red trails where they scrape his skin.

His mouth gapes open, but no sound comes out. It gapes and gapes and gapes, and it could swallow me whole.

Somewhere inside me, I drown and I wake and I drown again.

FORTY-THREE

Some people are like puzzles. You have to put the edges together first, work your way inside them. Mira is like that. But here in the darkness and the water, it does not matter how fast she swims up or how determined she is to find air for her burning lungs. It does not matter if she fights back. She will not be made whole again. Some people are built up to undo.

Devlin Gallagher is not a puzzle. He is not a mystery or riddle or enigma. Devlin is as straightforward as they come. He has been living inside his guilt for so long that he is made of it. It stains every part of him. It only takes seconds to see that he carries a guilt so heavy, so encompassing, there isn't much else left of him to find.

People often bury their guilt. They don't wear it out. But Devlin has been consumed by the events that brought his wife where she has been for the past two months. And here, back at the place that set her off, there is little else he has thought of for days, weeks, months even. The facts are these. Devlin killed his son. Accidentally, yes, but if that wasn't enough guilt to bury a man, he let his wife think it was her fault.

He is after all the one who fed the baby in the middle of the night, the one who without thinking placed him back in his crib on his stomach instead of his back. He was the one who said nothing when Maddie, sweet Maddie, woke up a few hours later and found that the baby wasn't breathing. Convinced that in her sleep-deprived state had she placed him in that position. She couldn't even remember her husband waking up in the middle of the night to feed the baby, could only rewrite and remember her own mistake. Devlin knew what he had done. Knew it as fact. And when he had the chance to ease some of his wife's guilt, he stood back and did nothing, too afraid that she would only see him as the man who killed their two-month-old son. Some days, he also felt like it was the only important part of him. Who could blame her if she felt the same? And so he kept his mouth shut and let her spiral into insanity. I, this room, these walls, had only fanned the flames that he had lit.

At the end of the room, Devlin sees his wife sitting on the floor, her legs bent beneath her. In her arms, she cradles something wrapped in a forest-green blanket. Maddie locks eyes with Devlin, her face impassive and cold, and peels back the edge of the fabric to reveal their unmoving little boy. Beneath the harsh light of the room, Devlin can see that his son's skin has a blue tint to it. His dead eyes stare up past his mother and focus on an unfurling corner of the wallpaper. Devlin's eyes follow and are caught by the floral paper and the way it seems to breathe. The marigolds blossom and wither in steady pulses, each petal alive. When he turns back, his family is gone.

For days, Devlin has felt the pull of the room. But last night, he found himself at the foot of the door almost as if it was out of his control. Almost. It was the only introduction the room needed. That was a taste.

This is the meal.

With Ellis, Devlin, and Mira here, the room begins to vibrate with possibility. Guilt is a scent that seeps from all of their bodies. It is potent and it is intoxicating. In Room 9, Devlin feels the crushing weight of what he has done. Feels the permanence of it.

He feels the loss of his son.

He feels the loss of his wife.

They pile on until it is all he knows. Soon, he begins to understand that this place is all that's left of them. It's a piece of the puzzle that makes up his wife. How will he ever know her whole when this piece is destroyed, if he still hasn't figured out how this room works or how he can save her from it? No. *Saving this room means saving Maddie*, I whisper.

A quiet part of him is in awe of the overwhelming magnitude of the room, a room that seemed wrong but subdued only last night. He is in awe of how quickly these feelings have come together, of how quickly he has made his decision. How certain he feels that it is the right one.

Devlin wonders if the room has a way of making him think what it wants, but he doesn't care when he feels the room is right. In reality, Devlin has lost any sense of what the room wants him to know, to feel, to face, and has fused his own convictions with mine.

Quickly, Devlin turns around and locks the door behind him. He glances at Mira, but his attention is firmly on the building fire, on the bed, and now the curtains, that have been set aflame.

FORTY-FOUR

Layla

"Devlin. What are you doing?" Ellis asked warily, like maybe he had misunderstood what he had seen. He stood firm in front of me and Mira, who was on the ground, her body still now, between convulsions. Devlin removed his jacket and used it to try to put out the fire. He barely looked at Mira when he walked in.

"We have to put the fire out. Help me," he said. Flame ran up the curtains. I could see it nearing the edge of the ceiling now as he tried to quell it. It was clear that he was going to be no help here. I needed to get Mira out. All of us needed to get out, and I wasn't going to let this psycho stop us.

"Devlin, we're leaving. If you'd like to stay in this burning room, you are welcome to," I said. I moved toward the door to unlock it, but he blocked me.

"Move."

"You don't understand," he pleaded. "This is all that's

left of her. I can't lose this place. Not until we understand what it did to her. How to undo it. Please." He was crying now. He frantically shoved his long hair away from his face and slammed his jacket against the burning bed again and again.

The flames on the curtains behind him were close to his shirt now. An inch from the edge of his sleeve.

With Devlin distracted again, I inched closer to the door, but again, he stopped what he was doing and blocked me. Angry, he gripped both my arms and pushed me back. For a second, I could see his eyes focus on something behind me. His furious glare softened into something else entirely, something tragic and broken. He closed his eyes.

"Please," he said again. I wasn't sure who he was talking to.

Next to me, I could see Ellis look back at Mira's slumped body as it began to shake again, writhing as if Mira was trying to get out of her own skin. We locked eyes for a second, and I saw him bend his knees. He nodded, almost imperceptibly, in Devlin's direction, and every part of me hoped I understood what he was trying to tell me.

"What's the plan here?" I asked Devlin, hoping to keep his attention on me. I took a few steps back, putting distance between us. The smoke was building, and it was getting harder to breathe. We needed to act fast. "Block the door until we pass out from smoke inhalation or burn alive, whatever comes first? There's no stopping this!" I said, motioning around us.

Before Devlin could answer, Ellis ran for him. He kept his body low, his arms tackling Devlin around the waist. They tumbled down. Devlin's head hit the door, hard. But before Ellis could wrap his arms around him and pin him to the floor, Devlin twisted away and pinned Ellis to the ground. It was a solid effort, but Devlin was taller, stronger, older. I could see his muscles tensing against the sleeves of his shirt. Ellis didn't stand a chance. Not alone.

I grabbed a glass picture frame off the wall and slammed it against his head. It shattered when it made contact, the edges of glass slicing my skin open. He stumbled off Ellis and groggily stood up, disoriented by the impact and the smoke and the fire. I backed up toward the bed, my hand leaving a trail of blood in front of me as I dropped the glass shards. When he was close enough, I curled my bloody hand into a fist and smashed it up against his nose.

"Fuck," he cried out as blood gushed down his mouth. His hands went to his face, trying to stanch the blood. I didn't know much about fighting, but I knew enough to keep my thumb untucked. Still, it hurt like a bitch. When his eyes watered, I slammed my knee into his balls. Just for added measure. He crumpled to the floor as he held his groin, moaning in pain. Before he could orient himself, Ellis came up behind him and slammed one of the empty glass bottles of orange juice into Devlin's temple. He was knocked out cold then.

"You okay?" Ellis said.

I nodded. I felt relieved, like I could breathe, but only metaphorically. The smoke was getting thick, and we had to get out of here.

"I'll get Devlin. You get Mira," he said.

"Why? He deserves to stay if he wanted to be here so badly."

"Layla" was all he said. I knew he was right. I knew we couldn't leave Devlin here. It didn't mean I needed to be happy about it.

"Fine."

I wound my arms beneath Mira's armpits and began to drag her out of the room. Her body was still now. I hoped whatever it was had passed.

Ellis flinched when he touched the doorknob. He wrapped the edge of his shirt around his hand and quickly opened the door for us, wincing even then.

I gulped in the fresh midnight air. Mira began to stir, and I felt instant relief that maybe, just maybe, she was waking up, that the love of my life wasn't dead seconds after I kissed her.

Ellis pulled Devlin out, letting his torso fall the few inches into the hard pavement with a thud. I could see the flames against the window now, but I smiled up at him, relieved that we had made it out, even if the fire was still going strong a few feet away. At least we weren't inside. But Ellis didn't smile back. He looked at me, long and hard, and I knew then what he was about to do.

"No. Ellis!"

He didn't say anything. He just stepped back into the burning room and quickly closed the door behind him.

FORTY-FIVE

Mira

There is blood beneath his fingernails, red seeping from the trails he made on his own throat. If air couldn't enter his mouth, Khalil would force it through another way.

But none of this feels right. I take a step back, unwilling to be lured in by whatever games the room is playing.

"I'm done. I'm not here. Not really," I tell the endless space.

Khalil stops his frantic mauling of his own throat and stares at me.

"Of course you are, Mira. Why wouldn't you be? You're here. Just like I am. Because of you."

I shake my head, trying to shake the image of him away. To wake myself from whatever hell this was.

"You did this, Mira. Don't you see that? You wanted so badly to survive, you didn't care that it meant I couldn't." He steps closer. With every step I take back, he places one foot forward.

"And now you get to live with that."

The closer he gets, the stronger the feeling of drowning becomes. His hands grip my arms, and I can feel his cold, clammy fingers against my skin, his fingernails digging into the backs of my arms. Slowly, his mouth opens. A thin stream of water spills. When he coughs, a piece of seaweed edges out. He doesn't look away when he sticks two fingers inside his mouth and pulls out the long dark green strand from the back of his throat.

He lets it fall, and I feel it land on my shoe. I can feel my panic rising, my heart racing; he is so close now, I can make out the freckles atop his decaying skin. The closer he gets, the more trapped I feel. The darkness begins to envelop us. I need to get out. But how do you fight the fucking shadows?

I already know the answer, though. To understand that they're just that.

I take a deep breath, ignore the salt water in the air, Khalil's rotting stench. I step back, and this time, he doesn't follow. This room latched on to my guilt and shame, and deep down, I know its hold is loosening.

"You don't have the power you think you do. Not over me." Khalil, the room, whatever this thing is, steps back. There is shock written on its face.

"I know what I did. He's gone. You're not him and he's

not you and I can't take any of it back. It'll always be a part of me. But I can't carry this guilt forever. And you can't keep using it against me."

With every word the surrounding darkness abates. It retreats back to its corners, and with it, Khalil.

I swim up for air. I reach for solid ground.

FORTY-SIX

If I have to burn, I won't be the only one. Ellis shuts the door behind him, locks it with a dead bolt and then, for good measure, the chain. He winces when his hand makes contact with the metal, but Ellis does not care. He feels the motel keys in his pockets and realizes he took them from the front desk without thinking, assuring his own death without ever meaning to. The room is hot and thick with smoke, and Ellis has a hard time making anything out. The bodies, though, are exactly where he left them.

The anticipation is nearly unbearable. Ellis walks past the beds, the nightstands, the desk, and enters the bathroom. He wants to take a deep breath, to ready himself for what he is about to see, but the smoke makes it impossible, and so he coughs and steps over the other two bodies in the bathroom to find his father, lying facedown on the cold tile. Ellis sits down next to him and holds his father's hand. If this is the end, then at least he can have the goodbye he always ached for. Ellis doesn't need to say anything. Being with his father, holding his hand, as cold as it is, brings him some of the peace he had hoped for. He knows now why his father has ended up here. Understands that the same guilt that lived in Noah lives in him. It's funny, he thinks, how different he thought they were. And now, here they are. He leans back, his head resting against the sink, and settles himself on the ground.

He wonders if the fire department will come before the fire spreads to the other rooms. He doesn't want his mother to lose everything, but there's always insurance, so he thinks she'll be okay. Even beyond the flickering of the flames, the dizzying smoke, Ellis can hear banging on the door, a shoulder being shoved against it, his name being called again and again, first by the girl and then eventually by a second voice that tugs at his heart. He loves Izzy, he thinks to himself. He never felt like an only child, because of her. He hopes that she knows this.

Ellis wonders if burning my walls, this room, will be the end of me. He decides that he will never know for sure. This, what he's doing, is not about the room. The flames against these walls were only happenstance. An open opportunity.

For Ellis, it is too late. He needed to pay for what he had done. Or more accurately, for what he hadn't done to stop me. Ellis could not deny that though he was not complicit in these eight deaths before him, he had not done enough to save those that came after. Months of guests, of lives, ruined. They might as well have been the bodies before him. What difference does it make?

The flames lick the wallpaper. They climb up the furniture. They reach the bathroom now. They crawl against the carpet until they meet tile, and then they swallow the wooden doorframe whole. It is quick and formidable.

Next to him, his father's body fades into smoke and back again. It is difficult keeping control. But as hot as they burn, these are only walls.

But then Ellis hears his mother's voice, and his heart falls into the bottom of his stomach.

"Elly," she screams again and again.

He did not think he would have to sit through this while his mother waited for him to die. He did not think any of this through. Why had he spent so much time angry at her? he wonders. Why did he have to blame her for all the pain he felt? Why did he resent her for wearing her grief differently than him? So many questions, and suddenly, all Ellis wants to do is put them behind him.

Slowly, Ellis stands up. He is no longer calm. His heart begins to beat loudly, erratically. This decision comes crashing into him, and he is suddenly reconsidering how much of it was his to make and how much of it was mine. The answer? You can't grow a plant where there isn't a seed.

And so, he says goodbye to his father, looks at the flames head-on, and runs clear through them.

They envelop him in a matter of seconds. He tries to pat them down, but the flames are crawling up his arms, his neck, and he can feel nothing but the heat, the piercing pain of it. Beneath the thick smoke of the room, he smells his own burning skin. In his panic, he twists and turns, trying to quell the flames, but now he is disoriented. He cannot make out the direction of the door, cannot see through the smoke and flames and his own burning skin.

Ellis does not make it out.

FORTY-SEVEN

Layla

"Ellis! Ellis, open the door!" I screamed as I pulled and twisted the locked doorknob, but it was hot to the touch, and Ellis was silent on the other side. We had made it out, damn it. We were in the clear. He *had* to go back in, had to listen to whatever the room was telling him. A few guests came out when they heard the yelling. They stood far away when they saw the flames. Some ran back to grab their things before the fire spread to their rooms too.

Finally, Izzy drove into the parking lot and jumped out of her car. She looked confused as she watched me bang on the door, screaming Ellis's name, but quickly connected the dots and started yelling for him too. I watched as she shoved her shoulder against the door, trying to force it open, but these old doors were stronger than they looked.

"I'll be right back. We have spare keys." Izzy ran to the front desk, and all I could do was wait. Devlin was still passed out cold on the ground a few feet away as I wiped the blood from Mira's face and waited for her to wake up. But then I remembered. Mira's jeans had pockets. Save for my camera strapped across me, all my things were still in the car, but Mira kept everything on her. I shifted her over, reaching into her pockets until I found her phone, and called 911. It felt like forever before anyone picked up.

"Nine-one-one operator. What is your emergency?" the woman on the line said.

"There's a fire at the Wildwood Motel. Someone is inside the room that's on fire. You have to hurry."

"We'll send someone now. What's your name?"

"Layla Saleh." The woman began to say something, but Mira suddenly gasped and I couldn't hear her anymore. I let the phone fall to the grass.

"Oh my God, you're okay," I mumbled into her hair as I hugged her. Her arms felt limp around me, but she sat up and hugged me back. If it wasn't for Ellis, everything would be all right with the world.

Izzy and his mother came back then. His mother ran to the door, started pounding at it.

"The keys are gone," Izzy told us. She sat on the ground next to Mira and me and clasped her hands over her head. I could see the tears streaming down her face, could feel her helplessness because we both felt it.

"Elly? Elly, open the door. Please, Elly. Don't do this. I

can't lose you both. Please." His mom started sobbing, barely getting the words out. She pulled at the edge of the window, but it didn't budge. We watched as she grabbed the heavy planter a few feet away and smashed it into the glass. It shattered, the planter landing inside the room, but the fire billowed out, a wall of impenetrable flames licking the curtains and now the only way in. Her knees caved and she found herself on the floor, her forehead against the warm door, waiting for her only son to respond.

He didn't.

FORTY-EIGHT

Mira

In the distance, we could hear the sirens wailing. Layla and I sat on the ground, watching the flames devour the room. Fire began to spread to the two rooms on either side, but by then, the red lights of the ambulance and fire truck had already lit up the wall of the motel. They would be able to stop it from burning to the ground. The bright flashing light tinted everything around us. I leaned against Layla and she rested her head on my shoulder. We stayed that way as the firefighters broke into the room. As they stood by and let coroners place Ellis on the stretcher, covering him with a sheet.

"Are you okay?" Layla said.

I nodded, not sure if I would start crying again if I started talking.

She squeezed my hand before she left to explain to a cop what happened. It didn't take long for them to hand-cuff Devlin and leave him in the back of a cop car. I could see him bawling in the back seat, his shoulders shaking, his cuffed hands tugging at his hair. They had to pull him away from the door when he wanted back in, to let the fire department through. Devlin immediately admitted to trapping us in the room, screaming about how he should be the one to die, how he had killed his own son, how he should be punished for what he did to his wife. It was enough for the cops to take him into custody.

I couldn't stop thinking about Ellis, about his mom and Izzy and how he felt like he had no choice but to go back to that room. I couldn't help but wonder what his final moments were like, if he passed out from the smoke before the fire got to him, if he regretted what he had done by the time it was too late to turn back. If he felt absolved of the guilt that tortured him so much he felt the only way out was to lock the door behind him.

Here, in the fresh air and ambulance lights, my own guilt felt lighter. It was still there, thoughts of Khalil resting on the perimeter of my mind, but it was different. I had spent the past few days so engrossed in these feelings. But now, now that I'd made it out, now that I was on the edge of believing that blaming myself did nothing, that the people around me still loved me even if it was taking me longer to come to terms with that, I could finally feel the guilt abating. Not entirely, sure. The image of Khalil next to me on the grass said as much. But he wasn't angry or dripping in salt water or crying for help. He just looked at me.

"I don't know how to forgive myself for what I did to you."

He didn't react, only looked at the fire, his quiet eyes watching the flames.

"I just know I need to," I said.

For a second, I let myself miss my brother as much as my body allowed. Let myself believe that he was here and that he knew I loved him, because I did, and that if I could trade places with him, I would. Khalil didn't say anything. He just stared at the flames, at the smoke rising, before he faded into smoke himself. Maybe I hadn't forgiven myself, but I was working on it. I knew I would. I knew I'd sit down with my parents after this and tell them everything that I had kept to myself for the past year. I didn't know if it would push them away or if we'd be able to finally grieve Khalil together, but I knew I couldn't accept what I had done and keep it from the two people who had loved him most.

Seeing Devlin still deep in his guilt—even when the room was falling apart at the seams, its walls and roof slowly caving in on it—made me realize that what I was feeling wasn't because the room and whatever made it come alive was gone. It was because of me. Because I had faced and accepted what I had done, when Devlin hadn't. Destroying the room could never end the torment of our guilt. We came in with it and we would leave with it too.

There was so much we didn't know about Room 9. If everyone in it was at risk because of the guilt and secrets they carried. If it chose people at random or called to people from far away. If it was really gone. But we knew what we needed to know, enough that maybe it wouldn't follow me out of here.

"How are you feeling?" Layla asked me as she sat back down. Her eyes were red. I could see trails in the soot on her face where her tears had been. "Should you see the paramedic, just in case?"

I shook my head. I felt fine. Scared, tired, broken. But fine. Maybe numb was a better word. A part of me was protecting the rest of me from understanding what had happened. Logically, I knew Ellis had never made it out of the room, but the part of me that needed to process that was numb to the news. Ahead of us, Izzy was consoling Ellis's mom, who was sobbing into her shoulder. Izzy held her tight, but she was crying too.

I didn't know what to do. There was nothing I could do for them. I couldn't bring back Ellis, couldn't un-let him into the room. I couldn't change what the room had done to him or take away whatever guilt he had carried with him.

I couldn't change the past, and as difficult as that was to accept, it was the only way any of us could move forward.

Ash rained down like snow, covering everything it touched. I let it rest on my skin, imagined it staying there for the rest of my life.

I leaned against Layla and held her hand. I knew we had a lot to talk about, but for now, she stroked my palm with her thumb and rested her head on my shoulder. Whatever came next, we would get through it together.

As the sun peeked over the horizon, we started our drive back home. The hours sped by, quiet except for the wind rushing past. When I dropped Layla off, she told me that she was off the waitlist, and for a few minutes, the hurt in my heart retreated.

"I'll see you in Chicago," she whispered against my lips.

"You know we have school on Monday, right?"

She rolled her eyes. "You know what I mean." Layla grabbed her things, squared her shoulders, and headed inside. What she had waiting for her was hard and messy and would take a long time before it would be made whole again. But I would be here on the other side of it.

I drove the two minutes back home. At my front door, I tried to borrow an ounce of Layla's bravery. It wasn't much, but it was all I could muster. My dad was inside, elbow-deep in dirty dishes, and when he saw me come in, he set the mug down. He was surprised when I hugged him, but a second later, he wrapped his soapy hands around me.

"Is Mom upstairs? I want to talk about something," I said, stepping back.

He nodded and left to get her. I stood alone in the middle of our kitchen. The sound of the forgotten rushing faucet and my quick heartbeat filled the space. Whatever happened next, I would survive it.

FORTY-NINE

The fire burns high, and I am being stripped of everything that I am. The wallpaper peels back as the flames lick its edges. The marigolds on the walls burn and wilt away until there is nothing left of them. The curtains collapse on the nearest bed, and within seconds, that too is engulfed in flames. These seams are coming undone. This place is withering before me.

But I am more than these four walls. More than this room and everything it holds. I exist beyond its boundaries. They think they can set me aflame and wait for the fire to do the rest? They don't know that I am made of their buried secrets and darkest thoughts. A match can't stand against those.

The Pull.

The room.

They are only extensions of what I am, what I am capable of. A body, a brain—they are not a being.

When they tried to understand me is where they went wrong. I am only made of the dark because the others were made of it too. There is no bias here, no fiction. There is only truth and then the rest. For decades, this place has found a way to survive. Why would this be any different? I am a guide to the dark, the road past the shimmering, simmering summer haze. Come closer and feel this heat.

I am more than a thing you can burn.

ACKNOWLEDGMENTS

Many would have you believe that writing is a solitary act. But if that were true, I wouldn't be sitting here, trying to properly thank all the lovely and brilliant people who had a hand in shaping this book, one way or another.

Chronologically, give or take, means thanking my parents first and foremost. I love you. Thank you for the many trips to the library. For pretending you didn't see me reading under the covers late into the night. For fostering and supporting my love of books. For saying *Of course you can* when I wondered if I could write them. It means more than you know.

To my sister and brother. I hope you know how much I love you both. Sarra, you hate it when I get sappy, but oh well, it's in print now for the world to see. Zyad, thank you for not drowning that summer, or for taking me down with you. I'm glad that this is fiction.

To Norma Rahal. I was thirteen when I met you and, up until then, had gone through life with an unremarkable definition of friendship. I quickly learned what it meant to find someone who truly saw you, who felt made of the same stuff as you. Thank you for reading every word, for wholeheartedly believing my dreams were inevitable, and for laying out the foundation of what it means to be a best friend. Without you, Mira and Layla would have nothing to build their love on.

To Kate Vinkovich, who said yes to being my Elena with only a twenty-minute heads-up, who is an endless stream of enthusiasm and support, who means more to me than I can ever say. I love you and I'm so lucky to know you. Thank you for existing.

Omar, the love of my life and father to our puppy. You kept me focused and motivated and reminded me that giving up wasn't an option. Thank you for the pep talks, the constant stream of snacks, and keeping Ronin entertained so I could write. I love you more than any words I'll ever find.

To Abi Inman. I remember our Brooklyn apartment with the ever-present leaks and occasional mice. I think back on it fondly now, in part because my thoughts settle on us writing on the couch as we paused to read scenes out loud. Thank you for being there for me. I'll follow you to any city.

Paul Griffin. Years ago, I met Paul when I was working on a book that I had nearly given up on. He gave me the push I needed to get it done and send it out to agents. And while I was waiting to hear back, I wrote this book, the one in your hands. Which is a long-winded way of saying, I wouldn't have gotten here if I never finished the last one. And that I owe to Paul. Thank you.

Nidhi Pugalia, who had an invaluable part in shaping this story. This would be a different book without you, and I am relieved I never have to know what that would've looked like. Thank you for the weekly writing sessions, for the lengthy discussions, and for understanding Mira and Layla on every level. I'll always be fortunate we found our way to each other. May the June of our friendship never come.

To my Vikings. Writing a book and being an editor is exhausting. But most days, you made work a place I loved. And even on the bad days, I knew I had a support system to lean on. I hope you know how much that meant. Thank you.

To Chloe Gong, who believed in my writing and gave invaluable advice on the book that came before. Thank you for the many emails back and forth, for being a part of the building blocks that got me to this story.

To Assil Hamdi for your lengthy voice notes, for answering all my questions, and for being so incredibly supportive and enthusiastic every step of the way. I'm lucky that we're family, but I'm even luckier that we're such good friends.

To Jennifer March Soloway, a dream come true of an agent. You saw something in this book, and in me, that I wasn't yet convinced was there. Thank you for being an incredible advocate and friend. I've said it before and I'll say it forever: I am so fortunate to have you by my side. Thank you for making my wildest dreams come true.

To Jess Harold, editor extraordinaire. I was walking along Central Park on an already perfect day when Jennifer called to say you wanted to acquire this. For years, I had imagined what that call would feel like, but that sort of joy is ineffable. Thank you for giving me that. And for giving this book a loving home.

To the incredible authors who had such kind things to say about this book: Aiden Thomas, Chloe Gong, David Arnold, and Jodi Lynn Anderson. I've long admired the way each of you craft books and it is a strange and surreal thing to know that you enjoyed mine.

A special thank-you to Norma Rahal, Mariam Alameri, Zyad Metoui, Omar Radwan, Teniece Roberts, and Kate Vinkovich for being my Mira, Layla, Ellis, Devlin, Izzy, and Elena. And, of course, to Abi Inman for being the best assistant director I could ask for. I loved doing this photo shoot just as much as I loved writing this book, which is to say a lot. You've let me bring these characters to life, and I am forever grateful for that.

And finally, to everyone reading these words. Thousands of books are published every year, and yet, here you are holding mine. I thank you. I hope you found this exactly when you needed it.

ABOUT THE AUTHOR

Meriam Metoui is a writer, book editor, and (when she has the time) a photographer. She is a graduate of the University of Michigan and Hunter College, where she received a master's degree in English literature. Born in Tunisia, she now lives in Detroit, Michigan, with her partner and puppy. *A Guide to the Dark* is her debut novel.

You can learn more at **meriammetoui.com** and follow her on Twitter and Instagram **@meriammetoui**.

CREDITS

Art and Design
AURORA PARLAGRECO

Audio
RECORDED BOOKS

Contracts
KAREN CHAU

Copyeditors and Proofreaders
JACKIE DEVER, JESSICA WHITE & ILANA WORRELL

Editor
JESS HAROLD

Managing Editor
ALEXEI ESIKOFF

Marketing
LEIGH ANN HIGGINS & NAHEID SHAHSAMAND

Production Editor
KRISTEN STEDMAN

Production Manager
JIE YANG

Publicity
TATIANA MERCED-ZAROU

Publisher
JEAN FEIWEL

Sales
JENNIFER EDWARDS, REBECCA SCHMIDT, NATALIA BECERRA,
JAIME BODE & JENNIFER GOLDING

School and Library Marketing
MARY VAN AKIN

Subsidiary Rights
KRISTEN DULANEY & EBONY LANE

ANDREA BROWN LITERARY AGENCY
Jennifer March Soloway, Alison Nolen, Kelli Stevens Kane & all the
incredible agents at ABLA who helped get us here.

UNITED TALENT AGENCY
Mary Pender & Orly Greenberg